seventeen

The Truth About

GIRLFRIENDS

by Amy Fishbein

HarperCollins*Publishers*

A PARACHUTE PRESS BOOK

Created and produced by
PARACHUTE PUBLISHING, L.L.C.
156 Fifth Avenue, Suite 302
New York, NY 10010

Published by
HarperCollins*Publishers*
1350 Avenue of the Americas
New York, NY 10019

For information write:
Editorial Manager, **seventeen**
850 Third Avenue
New York, New York 10022

Design by AFF Design
Cover photographs by Aimee Herring
Printed in Baltimore, Maryland by John D. Lucas Printing

Library of Congress Catalog Card Number: 200108672

ISBN 0-06-447243-4

9 8 7 6 5 4 3 2 1

First printing, May 2001

What Your Favorite Celebrities Say About Friendship

"**Friends inspire you** to become your best and still love you when you're at your worst."

—**Kirsten Dunst**

"Friendship means really caring about a person. Not just in a convenient situation. It means taking the time out to help that person when you have fifty thousand things to do. It means caring what's going on with that person, what problems they're having. It means really loving that person. **Friendship is love.**"

—**Leelee Sobieski**

Table of Contents

Acknowlegdments

Many thanks to Patrice Adcroft, Andrea Chambers, and my editor, Heather Alexander, for their support, encouragement, and guidance. Thank you to Melanie Mannarino, an ideal girlfriend without whom I could not have written this book. And thanks to Janet Laubgross, Ph.D., who gave me great insights for Chapter 9.

Introduction

What do you call a cheerleader, an advice columnist, a personal stylist, a security blanket, a diary full of your deepest secrets, and all your favorite stuff rolled into one?

Your girlfriend, of course!

Girlfriends are all those things to you . . . and more. They're your own personal pep squad—rooting for you, whatever you happen to be doing. They give you the right advice when you need it most, and you can always count on them for the coolest suggestions about clothes and hair.

They also keep you calm in stressful situations, would rather die than dish the dirt on you, and are ready at a moment's notice to discuss the best parts of your favorite song, TV show, movie—whatever!

This book is all about celebrating the awesome relationship you have with each and every one of your girlfriends. It's a relationship that becomes more and more important as life gets increasingly complex.

Let's face it: When you were a kid, the biggest dilemma you had was whether or not to share your periwinkle blue crayon with the girl at the table next to yours. Now you're dealing with school, family, guys, and your own weird, sometimes unpredictable feelings about them all. Who other than your best friends could make that bearable—or even fun?

Okay, so sometimes you and your friends hit a snag. You could have a fight, or a misunderstanding, or someone's feelings could get hurt—but, really, that's all part of the process. And hey, we've been there, so we can help you get past the speed bumps and back on the road to everlasting friendship.

Every month at **seventeen** we get hundreds of letters from readers who have questions about every aspect of friendship. We've included their letters in each chapter of this book. We also asked readers to share their amazing insight and weigh in with their own opinions and experiences throughout the book in sections labeled "Your Turn."

So, basically, **what you've got in your hands is the ultimate friendship road map**. This book will take you through it all, from how to grow even closer to your best gal pal, to how to fight fair over a guy. We'll also talk about everything from to how to deal with peer pressure to when to tell your friend what you *really* think.

So grab your gal pals, find a comfy spot, turn to page 1, and **let's go, girlfriends!**

LYLAS (Love You Like a Sister)

> **FRIENDSHIP RULE:**
> Best friends understand you better
> than anyone else. Sometimes they
> know you even better than you
> know yourself!

When everyday life gets weird or confusing, what's better than knowing you can count on your friends to understand exactly what you're going through?

No one can help you get through making a major decision, get over a bombed exam, or get past your own insecurities like one of your girls. Which makes total sense, because your friends are dealing with the same problems, situations, and emotions that you are.

1

Best Friends

But let's talk for a second about **the ultimate girlfriend** —the one who is *really* there for you. She's the one you call at three o'clock in the morning when you are in need of immediate counseling because your crush just ignored the Instant Message you sent him. She's that one special person in your world you call **your best friend**.

What distinguishes her from the rest of your buds? What is it about her that makes her most special to you?

Well, a best friend knows your strengths—and all the parts about you that you think are cool. But unlike everyone else, your *best* friend is someone you let in on your weaknesses, too. Which, let's face it, can be kind of scary.

But once you have that intense level of trust with another person—once you realize that all your deep dark secrets and insecurities are safe with her, you can be your most honest, real self around her.

Our point: Your best friend knows the essential, plain-and-simple you and (surprise!) she likes you just the same (or, actually, even more) for it. She knows you so well she can predict your moods (which is why she *never* calls to wake you up from your daily midafternoon nap).

More than any other girlfriend, you know that your best friend loves you—all of you, no matter what.

What I Like About You: Hand this book to your best friend! In the space below, ask her to write the top ten things about you that make you special. Then you can do the same for her.

What I Like About You:

1.
2.
3.
4.
5.
6.
7.
8.
9.
10.

What You Like About Me:

1.
2.
3.
4.
5.
6.
7.
8.
9.
10.

You know you can **depend on your best friend for anything at any time**. Like when you get into a blowout fight with your mom or sister, your best friend will no doubt agree with your point of view about the whole thing, and she'll suggest ways to settle the argument.

When something is really bothering you, like the fact that your little brother just flushed your pet goldfish down the toilet, your best bud will calm you down (and maybe take you to the pet store to find Goldy II). And when you do finally score an A+ on your Spanish exam, your best friend will be waiting for you afterward with a frozen mochaccino and an **"I knew you could do it"** smile on her face.

Your Turn

Best Friends

"I know that my best friend and I can tell each other anything, and we help each other out. We also know exactly how to make each other laugh." —**Vicky**

"My best friend is someone I can climb a mountain with, laugh over a magazine with, or simply sit and do nothing with." —**Gracie**

"Her sense of humor always brings me back to reality." —**Nancy**

"It's important to have my best friend there all the time, helping with little problems like home-work or big problems like death. Having that shoulder to cry on any time is special to me." —**Jenny**

"My best friend knows me so well that when we talk, I don't have to explain my past because she already knows about it or was there when it happened." —**Sara**

4

You two are best friends, attached at the hip. But how well do you *really* know each other?

First read the questions below out loud to your pal. While you mark down the answers you would choose, she should mark down what she thinks *you* would do in each situation on a separate piece of paper. Then, have your friend read the questions out loud, and reverse the process. When you're finished, find out how well you and your *prima chica* predicted each other's responses. For every answer that matches, give yourselves one point.

1 We're shopping at the mall. The minute we walk through the front entrance, I head straight for:

    A. the music store.

    B. the food court.

    C. the Gap.

2 At the last football game of the season, I spot my boyfriend by the concession stand talking to a cheerleader. I:

    A. immediately run out of the stadium, crying.

    B. walk right over to them and ask, "So what's going on here?"

    C. ignore it. He probably knows her from class.

3 It's finals week and I've got three superhard exams. When that slacker guy who never shows up for class

5

offers me the chemistry test answers at lunch, I:

   A. snatch them and memorize them by Thursday.

   B. take them, but then throw them out and decide to kick butt on the test the honest way.

   C. turn him down cold. I'm not getting busted for cheating.

4 **You borrow my favorite black turtleneck sweater to wear to a party—and accidentally rip a small hole in it. When you tell me, I:**

   A. can't even talk to you until I've calmed down.

   B. don't really care. The hole is on the seam, so my mom can probably sew it easily.

   C. let you know where you can get me a new one.

5 **In volunteer club after school, the senior class president humiliates me for my feeble effort to raise money for the downtrodden in New Delhi. What am I thinking?**

   A. Please! It's not like she did so much better with her "Benefit the Baby Llamas" bake sale last week.

   B. Oh my God. I *cannot* cry in front of all these people right now.

   C. Man! I'm such an idiot! Now they'll never let me organize an event again.

6 **We're at Applebee's. I'm in the rest room when the waiter comes to take our drink order, so you:**

   A. order me my usual: Coke with no ice.

   B. ask him to come back in a few minutes.

   C. order a Sprite and a Coke—whatever I don't want, you'll drink.

Scoring

8–12 points: In sync

What you two have is a rare thing. You know each other inside and out, up and down. You can finish each other's sentences and predict how you'll act in almost any situation. You're privy to the smallest details of each other's lives—not only because you're best friends, but because you're perceptive and pay close attention to each other, which are two key characteristics of a considerate pal.

3–7 points: On the same page

You're pretty in tune with each other, but sometimes, when it comes to certain details, you're a little off key. Don't despair! You can work with that—you've got a strong foundation for a close friendship! With a little more time spent together, you'll be in perfect harmony. In the future, remember to really listen to what your friend says, and observe how she acts in various situations. It will make you closer, better friends.

0–2 points: Off base

Hello—have you two met before? Take a little time to introduce yourselves to each other—right now. But seriously, wanting to be best friends isn't a bad place to start. Tight-knit friendships take time to develop. It's great that you like each other and think of each other as close pals. Now you just need to hang out and talk some more. Spend some time playing the fun get-to-know-you games in Chapter 5.

She's Your Best Friend

1 She's willing to give you the sniff test after phys ed, to tell whether you need more deodorant.

2 She finishes your sentences. (You: *The last thing I need right now*— Her: *—is another wise-guy remark about your funky hot pink pants?*)

3 You two can find laughter in anything: a nosedive off the curb, the birthday slippers your gram sent you, the fact that your boyfriend broke up with you the day before Valentine's Day.

4 You love Indian food. She hates it. To celebrate the fact that you made Honor Roll, she suggests going to the Taj Majal Buffet.

5 After overhearing her crush telling his pals how cute he thinks she is, you hop a bus across town to her part-time job so you can give her the news ASAP.

6 You spend a weekend visiting your dad, and when you get back, your e-mailbox is filled with updates from her.

7 When she tells you she's going to sleep-away camp for the entire summer, you're miserable, but not worried. When she gets back, you two will just have *plenty* to talk about.

2 chapter

Circle of Friends

> **FRIENDSHIP RULE:**
> Every friend, no matter how close she is, brings something different and special to your life.

In addition to your best friend, you probably have a **whole group** of other friends. Maybe it evolved this way: You and Jennifer met each other in pre-K. Then, in first grade, Stephanie came to school and you and Jennifer fought over who got to sit next to her at lunchtime. Finally, along the way, the three of you decided your lives wouldn't be complete without your next-door neighbor Veronica's classic cackle and fab sense of humor.

Now the four of you are as **inseparable as the chocolate and vanilla in a frozen yogurt swirl**. And you wouldn't have it any other way.

9

Your core group of girlfriends is important in so many ways. Each member of the group can bring out the best in you—whether it's by encouraging you to go out for the school musical, or by laughing at all your jokes. **Your best buds also make it easier to improve the person you are.** (Face it, you would you never have learned the breast stroke if your pals didn't take swimming lessons with you every summer since the third grade.)

Are some pals closer to you than others? Sure. In reality, you're only going to have a few (maybe two, three, or four) girls who will stick by you at all times—girls who you will consider your closest friends. But remember—**you don't have to be true blue buds with every girl you hang out with.** There are other kinds of friends, too.

You can always share a secret with your homeroom pal, your doubles tennis partner—or someone outside your tightly knit core of companions. In fact, in this chapter, we'll show you how you can have many different kinds of friendships with people. After all, the more, the merrier, right?

Confused about where some people fit into your life as compared to others? Don't sweat it. Chances are, all of your pals will fall into one of **three circles of friendship.**

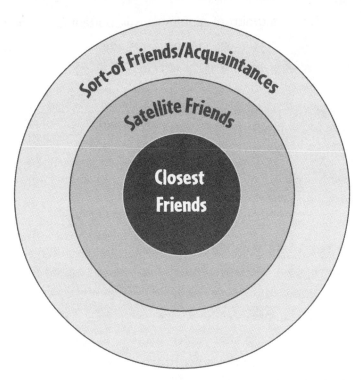

Take a look at the diagram above and let's work from the inside out. The **smallest circle** represents your *closest friends*—the girls you always hang out with. What these friends have in common is that they're all privy to many intimate details of your life. They each have a complete picture of you.

These buds are your top priority: You hang out together on weekends, celebrate each other's birthdays, and spend hours on the phone with them on a regular basis.

Directly following this group, in the **middle circle**, are the **"satellite friends."** These girlfriends orbit just outside your immediate girl group. These pals may know that your favorite color is orange, or that you hang at Vinny's Pizza after school (light on the sauce, extra cheese!). But they don't have a complete picture of you, not the way your core group does.

They aren't fully in the know regarding your most secret wishes and desires. But they can be like a breath of fresh air—giving you a new perspective on a problem, or turning you on to a kind of music that you and your buds don't know about.

Okay, **you wouldn't want to hang with your satellites 24/7, but that's cool.** Maybe the biggest thing you have in common—and the only reason you started talking— is that you both totally love chem lab.

Fine. If the great conversations you have with your lab partner continue long after you've figured out how to perform a litmus test, terrific. On the other hand, if next year, when chem's over, you only say "hey" as you pass in the halls, that's fine, too. It's the nature of the satellite relationship.

That doesn't make your time with your lab partner any less valuable, because, as we mentioned earlier, **through the years you'll have many, many friends, all of whom bring something unique and special to your life.**

So even though satellites may not be first on your phone list come Friday night, when you do see these pals, you know you'll have a blast with them.

Finally, in the **outermost circle**, are your sort-of friends, otherwise known as **acquaintances**. The girl who sits in front of you in homeroom, the tenth grader who rides the school bus with you every morning, your rival debate team's captain—any one of these people can be an acquaintance.

You'll probably have one very specific thing in common with each one of your acquaintances. (Usually it's that, by chance, you find yourselves scheduled to be in the same place at the same time.) But that doesn't mean you can't get in some quality talk time with these pals. For example, when you see your homeroom buddy toting around the latest thriller book, you might feel free to share your passion for the Sci-Fi channel and Ouija boards. When you admire the ultrashiny lip gloss your bus pal is wearing, you two could end up trading hair and makeup tips.

Even if you don't see or talk to your acquaintances until the next time you're scheduled to be with each other, **these friends are valuable!** They're sharing their opinions with you about stuff you care about. Besides, if you find yourself walking into a party by yourself, these are the friends you'll be happy to spot in the crowd.

RENT IT, SEE IT, LIVE IT:

Beaches. (1988-PG-13) Through love and hate, sickness and triumph, lifelong best friends CC (Bette Midler) and Hilary (Barbara Hershey) stand by each other.

What kind of friend is she?

Some people are naturally good listeners, while others are big-time talkers (you can hold the phone away from your ear for five minutes, and when you come back they'll still be chatting away). A healthy friendship should let all aspects of our personalities shine through, but there does have to be some give and take. **Do any of the friend types in the following chart seem familiar to you?** After figuring out which category your friends fall into, see if you can find your own type.

THE TYPE	WHAT YOU LOVE ABOUT HER	WHAT DRIVES YOU CRAZY
Lazy girl	If you don't call her for weeks, she won't get mad—because she hasn't called you either.	Though you know she loves you, if you don't make plans to get together, she won't do it.
Needy friend	She values your opinions and takes your advice to heart.	Sometimes you've got enough trouble deciding what you want for lunch, let alone planning her menu, too.

THE TYPE	WHAT YOU LOVE ABOUT HER	WHAT DRIVES YOU CRAZY
Bossy bud	On Monday, she's already decided what time your girl gang is going shopping on Saturday, and how you are getting there.	Her totally organized way of making social plans make you feel like a slacker.
Sometime friend	She pops into your life when you least expect it—with two tickets to the hottest concert of the summer.	She's often mysteriously absent just when you need her most.
Possessive pal	She calls you, she makes plans to hang out, and she meets you at the library to study.	She gets visibly jealous when other friends call you, make plans to hang out with you, or meet you to study.

Remember, even though your friends' styles can sometimes annoy you, girlfriends recognize that *a true pal's pluses outweigh her negatives.*

What's your favorite way to help a friend?

Having great friends is only half the equation. You've got to *be* a good friend as well. Your buds need you for support and love and a sense of fun as much as you need them. The way you choose to give that support says a lot about who you are as a person, and as a girlfriend. Take the quiz below to find out your help-a-friend style.

1 **Your best friend just called you to say her boyfriend dumped her. As she sniffles on the other end, you say:**

A. "You need to vent—tell me everything."

B. "I'm coming over—with Doritos, my sister's tarot cards, and videos."

C. "Here's what you have to do: Throw away *all* traces of him—pronto—and then write down all of your feelings in a journal."

2 **The American history final exam is tomorrow. Your friend needs to get a B or else she fails the class for the year. She calls you at 10 P.M. the night before, panicked. You:**

A. suggest she meet you at the bookstore café in ten minutes for a study break.

B. ask if she needs to run through the Civil War timeline with you over the phone.

C. help her map out a study strategy: She should read only the first and last two pages of each chapter, and then go over her class notes, highlighting key points in different colors.

3 Your pal has a difficult decision to make: Switch over to advanced classes and risk getting B's instead of A's, or stay in the regular classes, where she knows she'll do well. Your advice is to:

A. switch into advanced classes. It's the only way to get into a good college.

B. consider the pluses and minuses of advanced classes. Then, the two of you can talk things out together.

C. weigh her options and then decide for herself. This isn't something you can help with.

4 Your friend's dog, Peanut, just died. The best way to make her feel better is to:

A. bring her to the pound to pick out another precious pet.

B. let her talk about Peanut (how he licked her face every morning to wake her up; how he greeted her, tail wagging, when she got home from school every day) and how she'll miss him.

C. take her out to the movies and then a party where there'll be tons of cute guys!

5 Trauma! Your best friend just found out that her mom's new job might require a relocation. You know she really needs you to come over and:

A. calm her down, because you know she is freaking out, asking herself stuff like: How will she make new friends? Will you two lose touch? What will her new school be like?

B. help her get information on all of the cities she might move to, and make a real plan for keeping in touch long-distance.

C. talk about anything *but* the move.

13–15: The listener

You don't like to solve a friend's problem; you'd rather let her find the answers on her own. You've got a knack for listening sympathetically, whether a pal is on a tirade about her American history teacher's tough grading system or is gushing about her rebound crush. Your laid-back, nonjudgmental attitude calms your pals in high-stress situations, and allows them to solve their own problems, just by talking them through.

9–12: The good-time girl

"That's nothing a little fun can't fix" is your motto. Rather than solve her problem, you prefer to distract your pal with a good time. Sure, you know how to tread lightly when you deal with a weepy friend just been exiled to Dumpsville—but you also know that she can complain just as easily about that jerk at the local diner as she can alone in her bedroom closet. When your pals are sweating the serious stuff, they can count on you to balance their mood.

5–8: The advisor

You're an expert problem solver. You pride yourself on your ability to see the problem, assess it, and then solve it. You're no stranger to post-Dawson's phone calls from pals who need help studying, and you know exactly what to do when a friend loses a treasured pet. You've got an opinion, you think it's the right one, and you know it will help.

Juggling Acts

I have two different groups of friends. But I'm worried that some girls in one group won't get along with the girls in the other group. How can I spend equal time with everyone?

Having lots of friends to talk to and rely on is great, but it can be difficult, too—especially when you try to give each friend alone time and personal attention. **Juggling different groups of friends can get tricky.** Like when you have to ditch one group because you already promised the other one that you're theirs for the entire weekend.

One solution is to bring your various groups of friends together so that everyone can hang out *en masse*. Picture this: **You throw a huge end-of-year party, and you invite all your friends.** What could be better? **People from all different parts of your life will be in the same room at the same time.** Your best friend and her crew will be there, and so will your number-one bud from elementary school and her posse. Your lacrosse team and the drama club are hanging, along with your summer camp buddy, who's staying with you for the weekend!

Okay, we hear you freaking out. "This could be a nightmare," you're thinking.

In part, you're right. Who knows if your lacrosse teammates will find your best friend as loveably quirky as you do? And what if your melodramatic theater mates and your down-to-earth camp buddy end up at each other's throats?

We admit it, we can't promise that everyone will get along like one big happy family. But we can tell you that everyone will—at the very least—have a pretty good time. Why? Because of you, of course!

We pick our friends, in part, because they have a heavy dose of the same qualities we do. So if each of your friends has some of the same qualities you do, chances are that they'll all get along!

Even if you don't throw a party and invite every single one of your friends to it, you could find yourself in a situation where friendship worlds collide. How do you insure that everyone has fun and no one feels shunned? Check

seventeen READERS TALK ABOUT:

Juggling different groups of friends

"I have two different groups of friends, and those groups are broken up into even smaller groups. This is hard when I'm trying to plan my weekend. I try not to mix groups too much—instead I try to divide my time between my different friends."
—**Virginia**

"Most of my friends are in separate groups. But when one or two cross over, I just do the things that I normally do. Even if one person doesn't mesh well with the others, my friends are pretty intelligent and wouldn't be blatantly rude to someone else I'm friends with." —**Sarah**

out the different ways you can juggle any potentially sticky situation that might arise.

Juggling act 1: You can't choose whom to talk to.

Talk to everyone! Since you're the one person all your friends have in common, *you* have the power to bridge the gaps between different pals. First step: Make sure everyone knows everyone. Even if you're pretty sure that two of your pals met once at middle school graduation, introduce them again. Do this for all your friends. We guarantee it will reduce any potential awkwardness by at least fifty percent.

Juggling act 2: You don't know what to talk about.

Your buds might seem to have totally separate interests, but wait a second. **Think hard about things that your friends have in common.** Bring those topics into the conversation when you can. For example, say you know that Jessica has a huge CD collection and Alison sings lead for her new band. When you introduce them, say "Jessica, this is Alison. Alison just formed this awesome band." Then turn to Alison and say "You know, Jessica is really into music. She's got the hugest CD collection I have ever seen!" Then smile as the conversation takes off from there.

Juggling act 3: You want to spend time with everyone.

No doubt **you'll need to divide your time between your groups of girlfriends**, so if anyone in either of your groups starts feeling funny about you not sticking close to her, reassure her. Tell her not to take it personally if you can't spend intense, bud-to-bud time with her just now. Then **circulate**.

And, hey, while you're at it, **don't forget to have fun!** It can be cool when two different groups of your friends find themselves in the same place at the same time. If you have a blast while it happens, that's an extra guarantee that those around you will have a good time. And don't sweat it if everyone doesn't end up being best buds. That's not the point.

The point is for you to have a great time with all your friends at once!

So let's say an encounter between your groups of friends brings everyone closer together—is there such a thing as one girl gang being too close? Check out the next chapter to find out!

The Clique Effect

FRIENDSHIP RULE:
A girl gang can be a great
support system, but don't get so
wrapped up that you lose
your sense of self.

Okay, so you've got your girlfriends together, and you're all ultratight. So tight that you've noticed a few people referring to you as a **clique. The word gives you a weird feeling.** Should you be upset about it?

We realize the word "clique" has a bad vibe connected to it, but here's the straight-from-the-dictionary definition of a clique: "a narrow, exclusive circle or group of persons; especially one held together by common interests, views, or purposes."

So, what's the big deal about that? *Of course you want to spend time with people who enjoy the*

same things you do. For example, if you're really into sports and fitness, then you're probably going to pal out with girls who enjoy spending an afternoon in-line skating in the park, as opposed to girls who like being couch potatoes.

In other words, **don't let the whole clique thing make you crazy.** You and your athlete friends might seem closed off, but that doesn't mean that, in reality, you're not open to new friendships.

The same rule applies when you're on the outside of a clique. **Chances are, the girls you think of as unapproachable are just good friends with a common interest** (like cheerleading) who know each other backward and forward. Don't hold their friendship against them. And don't be afraid to go over to them if you're on a free period in the cafeteria and have nowhere to sit. You may be surprised by the friendly reception you get—especially when they realize you are just as into the latest boy band as they are.

But you have to be careful. **Sometimes good cliques can go bad.** How? When they become more and more exclusive, and you and your gal pals start to close yourselves off to making new friends.

Have you ever wanted to hang with someone (a guy, a girl, even a cool new teacher) but were afraid to do it because of what your girlfriends would think? Ever find yourself or your friends harshing on someone outside your group simply because she wasn't enough like you?

Maybe it's time to step back from the crowd and **consider how people from the outside might view you and your pals.** Does your girl group come across as too exclusive?

Think about why you wouldn't date that cute but slightly nerdy guy from your social studies class. Is it only because of what your friends might think? If so, maybe it's time you considered a break from the pack.

Make an effort to **expand your circle**. Sit with a different crowd of people at lunch once in a while, and don't take part in a collective stare-down when the new girl accidentally drops her books in the stairwell. People will think of you as a nicer, more approachable person, and trust us, that can only help make you more popular in the end.

Clique Caveats

My friends love to sneak out at night and do things their parents wouldn't normally allow them to do (we're thirteen and fourteen). I don't feel comfortable doing these things, but my friends keep pressuring me to go along with them. What should I do?

As we mentioned before, a clique can sometimes become more of a negative force than a positive one, especially when you find that the clique is taking over your identity. (Yeah, we know, it sounds like a bad science fiction movie—but it happens!)

Below, check out the three most common ways that a clique can lose its fun. We've also come up with some ideas about how you can handle it if it happens to you.

Clone Syndrome

THE PRESSURE: Your friends want to sneak out at night, or smoke, or drink, or hang out with a crowd you don't like—basically, they want you to join in on something they like to do, even if you're not comfortable with it.

HOW TO DEAL: This isn't as tough as you might think, because even though your friends may think you should, you don't have to join in on *everything* they do. Tell them, "I don't think I want to go with you guys to that party." And make up an excuse if your friends keep asking you why you're not coming along. Say something like "I have a major test in history tomorrow and I *have* to get my zzz's" or "My big sis is hanging with me that night." Even if you don't come right out and say it, your friends will get the picture that you're not totally hip with what they're doing.

WHEN TO DITCH: If your clique continues to pressure you, tease you, or even threaten not to be friends with you because you're not doing exactly what they do, that's the green light for you to go out and find another crowd. A group of friends who accept you for who *you* are and understand that what *you* think is important. Don't ever let anyone make you feel like you're uncool for not wanting to follow the flock.

Stick Like Glue

THE PRESSURE: Your pals expect you to be friends only with them, and they get angry when you hang out with girls outside your exclusive group.

HOW TO DEAL: Closing yourself off to new friendships makes no sense. If your pals are giving you a hard time because you want to hang with the new girl in your P.E. class, reassure them. Try saying "I really like being with you guys—you know you're my *closest* friends." Then take a stand. Say something like "But Laura is pretty cool, too, and I'm inviting her over tonight."

WHEN TO DITCH: If your friends deliver an ultimatum (as in "Either she goes or we go"), then it's time to call it quits. The fact that your group wants to be seen only with certain people is a neon sign saying that they are completely insecure—not only about themselves, but about your friendship. (They could be worried that you'll like your new pal better than you like them.) By demanding that you stay loyal to them, your pals are taking their lack of confidence out on you, which is a bad scene, no matter how you look at it.

Cookie Cutter Clique

THE PRESSURE: Every time you wear your favorite patterned tights to school, your pals refuse to be seen with you in the hallways. And after you tell them you are *so* over boy bands (or express any opinion that may be different from theirs), they start giving you the silent treatment. Basically, your friends want you to dress, act, and even think the same way they do.

HOW TO DEAL: Point out the plus side of having different taste in clothing, music, or guys: "I know we don't agree on everything—like my tights—but that's what makes us unique. Why should we all be exactly the same?" Fitting in with a group of friends should be a natural thing. You shouldn't have to play dumb in class to be cool, or pretend to love classic rock if you're really more of a pop music diva. Be yourself, and find friends who like you for you.

WHEN TO DITCH: Even if they sometimes need a little reminder that individuality is a good thing, true friends will accept (and appreciate!) your differences. So if you're trying too hard to get your friends to approve of your interests, or you find yourself changing those interests to accommodate your clique, get out now! Before it's too late!

You've Outgrown Your Clique

1 For the third weekend in a row, the other three girls in your group went out to the movies, and you decided to make it a Blockbuster night.

2 You've had a crush on Jeff, the hottie from business class, for weeks, but you're afraid to tell your pals because you're worried they'll think he's too geeky.

3 The self-proclaimed leader of your girl group has taken to laughing at the overweight girl in gym class—and you're not finding anything funny about it.

4 You find out on Thursday that your pal is having a party Friday night. When you ask her about the last-minute notice, she replies, "I guess I forgot to mention it. Come if you're not busy."

5 You'd rather take your little brother miniature golfing than spend yet another afternoon gossiping at your girlfriend's house.

QUIZ

Do cliques rule your life?

We've all had girlfriends who've felt the need to call every person in their clique before getting dressed for school. Have you reached that level of dependence? Find out by taking this quiz.

1 While shopping with your three best buds, you spot a pair of fabulous leopard-print boots. As you try them on, a pal remarks, "I wouldn't be caught dead in those." As the others agree, you:

A. shrug and smile, as you walk to the register in your new boots.

B. say, "Really? Are you guys sure? I think these are hot."

C. take off the boots, saying, "Oh, I know! I just wanted to freak you guys out."

2 Your childhood best friend, who moved away in fourth grade, is back in town for one night. That happens to be the same night your friends are having their annual pajama party. You decide to:

A. tell your pals the deal, and ask if there's room for one more sleeping bag in the family room.

B. tell your old pal that you've got plans at night, but can hang out all day.

C. invite your out-of-town pal to the sleepover. You're so psyched that your girl gang will finally meet your childhood friend—even if they're not expecting her to show up.

3 The drama department is holding auditions for the spring play. You've always wanted to act, but you've never told your girlfriends—they think drama is for nerds. So you:

A. decide against trying out. You probably wouldn't make it anyway.

B. tell them about your secret dream to be an actress. Maybe you'll change their idea of what kind of people go out for drama.

C. show up for auditions. If you do get a part, you'll just have to break the news to your pals.

4 The geeky guy in your algebra class asks if you want to go over formulas during free period. You say:

A. "Sure, meet me by my locker." You've never realized it before, but he's got amazing green eyes.

B. "No way." You just do not hang out with guys like him.

C. "Sure, but let's meet in the reference section of the library, okay?" None of your friends will look for you there.

5 Your mom loves shopping at the "everything for a dollar" store. Every Saturday she scours the place for outrageous bargains. When she asks you if you want to tag along this morning, you think:

A. "Maybe—if they have a location on the other side of town."

B. "Cool. I need a new lamp and throw pillows for my bedroom."

C. "No way. What if my friends see me?"

Scoring	**1.** a) 3	b) 2	c) 1	**4.** a) 3	b) 1	c) 2
	2. a) 2	b) 1	c) 3	**5.** a) 2	b) 3	c) 1
	3. a) 1	b) 3	c) 2			

5–8: Overruled!

If your pals don't approve, you don't either. You'll skip a shopping trip with Mom if you think it'll make you look uncool. You give your affection only to clique-approved guys. And you run your clothing purchases by your panel of pals before forking over cash for the items. **It's nice to have a group of girlfriends as a sounding board, but you're in danger of losing your sense of yourself.** *Take a second and think: What do you like? What do you want? It's important to develop your own individual tastes and interests. You have every right to be a leopard-boot-wearing, bargain-clothes-shopping stage actress who studies with geeky boys. And remember: You are at your coolest when you are being true to yourself.*

9–12: By the rules

You value your friends as trusted companions, not rulers of your life. It's nice being able to double-check with your buds when you're feeling indecisive, but whether or not they think animal prints are in this season, you'll still make up your own mind. And that's the way it should be. **When you really feel strongly about something, you won't let someone else's opinion stop you.**

13–15: Rule your own life

You're definitely your own person. You like to hang with your pals, and may have lots in common with them, but **nobody else influences what you do, think, or say.** *If you want to walk down the hallway holding hands with the geekiest boy in school, nobody else's opinion will stop you. And when an old friend shows up on a Saturday night, you don't ask your friends if she can crash your existing plans— you just bring her along. It's great that you are so strong-willed and confident. But* **don't forget to listen to and respect your friends' opinions,** *even when you disagree with them. A major part of any strong friendship is valuing what your pals say and think.*

Now that you're clear on the clique front, we're ready to move on. Next up, what happens when you and your chicas find yourselves on oppposite sides of an argument?

RENT IT, SEE IT, LIVE IT:

Never Been Kissed (1999/PG-13). Grown-up Josie Geller (Drew Barrymore) is researching high school life for a newspaper article she's writing. She goes undercover as a student and tries to fit in with the coolest girls in school, but Josie soon learns that the cool clique isn't all it's cracked up to be.

Friendship Roadblocks

> **FRIENDSHIP RULE:**
> If your friendship is on the rocks,
> communication is the only way
> to smooth things over.

Even if you and your best buds are tighter than a brand-new pair of leather pants, it's normal to go through periods when you're less than thrilled with one of your girls. **Fights happen**, and they can be set off by a whole bunch of issues. Your friends may spill a secret, hurt your feelings, or act insanely jealous of your new fall wardrobe.

Whatever the reason, you end up exchanging harsh words—and it seems as if your friendship will never be the same again. But actually, **more often than not, the problem is totally solvable**—if you handle it the right way. (And just so you know: Launching into a screaming match before school is *not* the right way.) Lucky for you, we've got solutions to practically any friendship roadblock you may come across.

Spilled Secrets

I told my friend that I liked this guy at school. By the next day, my crush knew. And he said my friend was the one who told him! How can I get her to stop blabbing my secrets?

If you share something totally classified with one of your girl-friends—like your daydreams about the hottie who sits next to you in fourth period—**according to the unwritten rules of friendship, girlfriend should zip it** and keep the info to herself. But when that doesn't happen—and your fourth-period hottie starts giving you goofy grins—it can be beyond mortifying.

You could make it a habit to specifically say "Please don't tell anyone!" before you unload major information to a pal. But delivering constant reminders about keeping things in confidence gets pretty tiresome. To make sure this never happens again, **when a friend spills a secret, talk to her about it ASAP.**

First of all, ask her how (and why) she let your secret slip. Was it an accident? (Maybe your crush looked over her shoulder when she was reading a note from you about him.) Was she trying to help you out? (What if she was playing matchmaker?) Or was it just a clumsy slip of the tongue?

Chances are your pal didn't mean to make you mad, and when you tell her how upset and embarrassed you are, she'll probably apologize.

On the other hand, if your pal doesn't seem like she cares that you're upset, and you think that she *intentionally* revealed your secret, there are probably other issues going on.

Ask yourself if you've been guilty of revealing her personal info lately, or if she could be jealous of you for any reason. Ask her about any unresolved issues you can think of that may have caused her to act this way. As difficult and frustrating as it may seem, it's important to get to the true reason behind her slip-up.

Oops! I Did It Again.

Of course, if you are the offender in a betrayal of trust, you should **be completely up front about your mistake.** Instead of getting defensive or angry, explain exactly where you were coming from.

If it was a well-intentioned slip, let your friend know you really thought you were helping. If it was an incredibly thought-less accident, admit it, and tell your pal you'll try harder next time to earn her trust. If you make good on that promise, then in all likelihood she'll forgive you as easily as you would forgive her if the tables were turned.

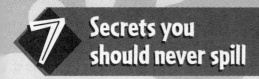

1 Your best pal still has a poster of the gang from *Boy Meets World* in her bedroom.

2 The last time she went on the roller coaster at Six Flags, she lost her lunch on the guy in front of her.

3 When she was in fourth grade, she stuck a raisin so far up her nose, it had to be removed at the emergency room.

4 Her favorite singer is '80s teen pop princess Debbie Gibson.

5 If she were stranded on a desert island, she'd bring her tattered blankie, her footie pajamas, and the entire *Little House* book series.

6 Her mom used to sew your friend's name into her underwear—and still does.

7 Her first kiss was with that geeky guy in school who snorts when he laughs.

Brutal Honesty

Sometimes it's easy to figure out exactly when to tell a friend the truth (like when she has a poppy seed between her teeth) and when to protect her from the cold hard facts (like when you find out her crush called her a cow).

Other situations can be harder to deal with. You may find yourself wondering, **Should a true girlfriend always be totally honest?** Or should she try to spare her bud's feelings?

We've noticed that our best girlfriends do a little of both. And the way they decide what to say is by figuring out exactly what they'd want to hear if the situation were reversed. Check out the following scenarios to see when the truth is better left unsaid:

- -

TRICKY SITUATION: Tryouts for the school play are coming up, and your friend's been practicing for auditions 24/7. The thing is, the part she's going for requires singing, and in your opinion, **she's no Britney Spears.**

TELL HER THE TRUTH: Nope. **Support is what she needs, not a critique of her crooning skills.** After all, it is possible that her off-key warbling has a charm you just can't appreciate. (Think everyone liked Macy Gray at first?) And even if she doesn't snag the part, she'll probably have a blast during tryouts, anyway.

TRICKY SITUATION:
You and your best friend are on a shopping spree. She comes out of the dressing room wearing a pair of jeans that **make her butt look huge.**

TELL HER THE TRUTH:
Break it to her gently, by saying something like **"Maybe I just don't like you in boot-cut jeans.** I'll get you a pair of reverse fit." As her friend, you've got two responsibilities here: 1) to keep her from making an unwise purchase and looking ridiculous; and 2) to tell her the truth without hurting her feelings. It's a delicate balance, but an important one.

TRICKY SITUATION:
Your pal is so nuts about her new boyfriend, **she thinks he's Ben Affleck and Matt Damon rolled into one.** But you just heard from his ex-girlfriends that he's got a nasty habit of dumping girls after dating them just three weeks!

TELL HER THE TRUTH:
Yes, yes, yes. But keep in mind that she's head over heels for him. Say something like "I know you're really into Jeff, and I'm so happy for you. I just want to let you know what I heard." **Fill her in on the hearsay, and encourage her to talk to him about it directly.** Don't offer advice ("Dump him before he dumps you!") unless she asks for it. After all, those exes could be carrying around a major grudge—and looking to stop your bud's new relationship before it has a chance to develop.

TRICKY SITUATION:
While changing out of your volleyball gear in the locker room, you overhear the goalie on the soccer team telling her teammates that **your friend has bad breath**. The next day, the same friend suggests that you both invite the goalie to have lunch with you.

TELL HER THE TRUTH:
Nope. There are other ways to solve this problem (the goalie's nastiness and your friend's odor issue) without giving it to your bud straight. **Tell her that you don't really trust the goalie, since you overheard her dissing someone** she's supposed to be friends with. And in the future, keep a stash of mints and gum on hand to offer to your pal. Pull them out and make a general observation like "Man! That cafeteria food is killer on my breath!" Then pop a mint into your own mouth. Chances are, your friend will take a mint—and the hint.

TRICKY SITUATION:
Your best friend loves to wear tight clothes — the more revealing, the better. You don't care what she wears, but now **people at school are calling her a slut.**

TELL HER THE TRUTH:
Nope. There's no need to tell your pal that everyone's harshing on her wardrobe. Style and fashion sense are completely subjective. If she's into V necks and tight pants, that's her business. But when you hear classmates mistakenly

labeling her "slutty," speak up and defend your pal. **Point out that the kind of clothes a person wears has nothing to do with whether or not that person is promiscuous.**

If you think your friend's outfits are misrepresenting her personality, try to get her to mix things up a bit. When she reaches for yet another fitted baby tee, pull a different style from the rack and say "You have so many shirts that look like that one. Try this one on—it'd look great on you." But remember, you can only try. She's free to dress however she chooses.

Malicious Gossip

I was friends with this girl until she began telling stories about me that weren't true—like I was making out with all of these guys when I really wasn't. Why would she do something like that?

There's no denying that it's fun to dish with your girlfriends. But unfortunately, **everybody at some point has repeated something that should've been kept under wraps**—or that isn't 100 percent true.

Girlfriends spread rumors for many reasons: to make a dull story sound more exciting, out of revenge toward the rumor victim, out of insecurity about themselves, or even because they think that knowing all the dirt will make them more popular.

In our opinion, the only thing to do in a case like this is to confront your gossiping gal pal, and ask what gives.

Maybe she's mad at you about something and decided to ruin your reputation instead of addressing the problem face-to-face. Or maybe she was trying to impress a bunch of seniors by embellishing a mildly interesting story at your expense. **Whatever her reasons, you need to hear them.**

TALK IT OUT.

When you do, no matter what her reasons are, resist the urge to scream, yell, or threaten to spread equally horrible rumors about her. Instead, communicate. Talk it out. Tell your bud that you really value her friendship, but that what she's doing is hurting you—big-time. If she can't offer up a reasonable explanation for her behavior, take a step back and evaluate your friendship. Ask yourself how strong your tie to this person is—and whether she's worth calling a friend.

What if *you've* got gossip you can't keep inside? If you're absolutely dying to share the latest dirt with someone, tell your mom, your diary, your cat—or try one of our favorite tricks: **tell a friend who lives in another town and doesn't know anyone involved.** That way, you'll feel like you unburdened yourself, and you'll know your faraway friend won't spread the gossip.

Basic Ground Rules on Gossip and Rumors

Whenever you're tempted to spill a juicy tidbit, don't repeat it if:

1. You're not sure that it's true. The longer it takes you to explain how you heard something, the less likely it is to be true (as in: My best friend's sister's boyfriend's brother heard from this kid who knows this girl who's going out with this guy who saw it all happen).

2. It involves problems in someone's family. Family traumas and scandals (think divorce, alcoholism, infidelity) are difficult enough for the person involved. Don't make the situation worse by having classmates gossip about it.

3. You know someone will get seriously and needlessly hurt if this information gets around. Maybe the captain of the football team doesn't know you saw his girlfriend kissing another guy while he was away with his family for Christmas. That doesn't mean you should fill him in on what happened by spreading the dirt around the school.

4. It's malicious. Spreading stories that unfairly make someone appear mean, dishonest, or promiscuous to the majority of the school is just not right. Keep secrets like that under your hat—or you can seriously ruin someone's reputation.

You're a Gossip Queen

1 You spy the substitute teacher smooching the head of the science department at 12 P.M. By 1:30, your entire English class has heard they're engaged.

2 You're dishing details about the love life (or lack thereof) of some girl you've never spoken to.

3 You get home from school, and before your backpack is off, you're e-mailing thirty of your friends to tell them that the homecoming queen let out an earth-shattering Diet Pepsi belch on the bus ride home.

4 Monday morning, you tell people at school how your friends got swept downhill in a flash flood this weekend. (The truth, of course, is that their outdoor camping trip got rained out.)

5 When a classmate wants to spread the news of a huge weekend party, she comes straight to you.

6 Friends note the evil gleam you get in your eyes every time you pick up some new and unspread info.

7 You find your mouth on automatic pilot. You can't stop yourself from beginning every sentence with "Did you hear. . . ."

QUIZ

How jealous are you?

A little competition between pals is often healthy and can drive you to succeed at your own goals. But when a pal gets an award that you both went for, your **competitiveness can give way to uglier feelings of jealousy**.

It's normal to feel envious every once in a while. But there is a fine line between being competitive and letting jealousy rule your every move. Do you cross that line? Take this quiz and find out:

1 **You and your bud went out for the volleyball team. You find out that she made it, but you didn't. You:**

A. are so upset that you don't talk to your pal for a few days. How could she even accept the position when you didn't make the team?

B. feel very disappointed and pout the rest of the day. But you tell your friend that you're really happy for her.

C. immediately give your friend a huge "Congrats" hug. You'll make it next year.

2 **It's two weeks before the prom, and your best bud tries on her black sequined dress for you. She looks absolutely fabulous in it. You say:**

A. "That dress looks pretty good on you, but maybe you'd look better in pink satin." (You don't want her looking better than you at the biggest party of the year!)

B. "I wish I could look that good in a dress like that. You look so pretty."

C. "You look so great! You'll be the prettiest one at the prom!"

3 Your family is staying at the Econo Hut on a Florida beach for spring vacation. A girl you're friendly with from school is going to the same beach, but is staying at the mammoth five-star resort next door. She asks if you want to hang out on vacation. You:

A. say no. You don't want to hear her bragging about her five-star digs.

B. tell her you'll call her hotel when you get there. You're not sure if you'll be able to tolerate your room once you see hers.

C. say yes. You can't wait to get iced tea hand-delivered to you while your toes are nestled in the sand.

4 Your best friend tells you that the hot new guy in homeroom just asked her out. You say:

A. "Really? Was he joking?"

B. "Cool. But don't forget about *our* plans to go to the movies Friday night."

C. "Awesome. I'll help you pick out what to wear."

5 Your pal gets picked to sing a four-minute solo in the annual choral concert. You had hoped the director would pick you. You:

A. are so upset that you refuse to stand next to your pal in rehearsals and consider not singing in the concert.

B. tell your friend how happy you are for her, then ask the director if she would please consider you for the next solo.

C. are glad that your pal's the one who got the part. She's got a better voice, anyway.

Scoring

Mostly A's—Green with envy

*You're so envious that you get mad at your friends when they have good fortune and you don't. Often jealousy stems from insecurities you have about yourself. So **try to remember what's fabulous about you.** Maybe your friend made the volleyball team, but you do stellar work on the yearbook. Part of being a good friend is being happy for your pals when they get a perfect score on a test even if you didn't. Because one day you'll have your own shining moment, and you'll want your friends to be happy for you in return.*

Mostly B's—True blue

*Sure, you feel bad when a pal gets asked out on a date, but you know how to keep your envy in check. A good way to nip jealousy in the bud is to talk with your pal about your feelings. For example, if the two of you are up for the same part in the school play, **let her know that you don't want the competition to come between you.** That way, your pal knows you're not only thinking of yourself, but of her feelings and your friendship, too.*

Mostly C's—Mellow yellow

*Jealousy? What's that? People as good-natured and selfless as you are hard to find. You have so much confidence that it doesn't matter if your friend got a fab new prom dress and you don't even have a date. But **if you are feeling a little jealous, it's okay to admit it**—to yourself and your friend. There's no crime in saying, "I'm so glad you're going to the prom. I hope I get asked, too."*

RENT IT, SEE IT, LIVE IT:

Circle of Friends (1995/PG-13). Benny (Minnie Driver) and her pals survive jealousy and betrayal, and learn the importance of forgiveness.

So now you know if you're the jealous type. If so, you're fully armed to guard against letting those ugly little feelings get in the way of your friendships.

But **what happens when you sense that a friend is jealous of you?** Follow this quick and easy game plan: Set aside some time to hang out—just the two of you. Then subtly remind your friend of the talents, traits, and abilities about her that you admire.

Say something like "You know, people may really like the way I sing, but I sure wish I could make people laugh like you do." Chances are, your friend will feel more secure about herself after a little pep talk—and the jealousy between you will vanish into thin air. That is . . . if the jealousy isn't over a guy.

Friends Come First

FRIENDSHIP RULE:
Boys may come and go,
but girlfriends are forever.

et's be honest. Most girlfriends love talking about, swooning over, and scheming to snag themselves a boy! But while hunting for a boyfriend is a group sport, **actually having a boyfriend is really a one-on-one situation.**

As a date or two with the hot guy from the tennis team develops from a news item into a more serious thing, you could find your relationships seriously tested. Especially if some of the members of your group have boyfriends and others don't.

Jealousy, loneliness, and unfriendly feelings can infect even the healthiest ties with your best buds. But that doesn't have to happen! That's why we've devoted this section to wiping any and all boy-related viruses out of your girlfriends' systems.

Reasons Girlfriends Are Better than Guy Friends

1 Only a girlfriend would discreetly pass you a maxipad in the lunchroom.

2 When you finally kiss your crush, your girlfriend won't mind hearing the details about it every hour on the hour.

3 Your mom never objects when your girlfriend invites you to sleep over at her house.

4 Whether you're talking about the hairstyle you want or the argument you've had with your little sister, when you ask your friend, "Do you know what I mean?" she always does.

5 If you burp in front of her (oops!) she won't suddenly find you less attractive.

6 When you come across your Barbie collection in the back of your closet, she's up for dusting them off for an afternoon of reminiscing.

7 She'll jump up next to you on your bed to croon old Spice Girls songs into your curling iron.

Contagious Crushes

My best friend and I happen to like the same guy. Lately, he's started paying more attention to her, and it's making things weird between us. Should I tell her the truth about how I feel?

A guy doesn't even have to reach boyfriend stage before he starts stirring things up between you and a pal. **When the two of you find yourselves seriously yearning for the attention of the same person, trouble is probably not far behind.**

It can be fun at first, trading notes and secret sighs about him—but things can turn sour as soon as the guy starts to show signs that he likes one of you. In a heartbeat, what was at first a fun diversion makes you feel anxious—like you're suddenly in a competition—and *she's* winning!

But hold on! That's antigirlfriend behavior (even if, we admit, we may have felt that way once or twice ourselves). It's totally counterproductive to let negative thoughts—*"Why is he going for her and not me? Is she prettier, smarter? And what does she have that I haven't got?"*—run through your head.

Why? Because, trust us, **the friend who's got the attention of the boy in question is feeling weird about the whole thing, too.** *She's* thinking, *"What if she hates me because of this? I'm psyched that he's interested, but why me? Should I ignore him so we'll be okay?"*

The two of you could go around in circles like this in your heads for eternity! Ridiculous, right? So how do you **stop the mind games?**

First, don't be tempted to demand that your friend not date the guy. It really isn't fair for you to ask your friend to give up an opportunity for romance. Remind yourself that you both liked him, and that it's pretty exciting that one of you may have finally caught his eye.

Second, acknowledge (and this may be really hard to believe, so you'll have to trust us) that **if this particular honey fell for your friend, then he wasn't the guy for you anyway.** Say it once in your head to convince yourself, and the second time out loud to convince your friend. It will make things much more comfortable between you in no time flat.

Okay, now **let's turn the tables**: Say this guy's flirting with you and not your pal. We've got a couple of ways to handle that situation, too. First, **be considerate** of your friend's feelings. Remember she was looking for love, too. Don't do a victory dance in the cafeteria, and don't start writing his name and your name "4-E"—surrounded by little hearts—all over everything you can get your hands on.

Second, **be up front** and don't consider dating the cutie on the sly—it may seem like it will keep the peace in your relationship, but it won't solve the problem. Especially if she finds out you're being less than honest. Instead, confide in her that he asked you to the movies this weekend. Tell her that you really want to go, and you'd like to fill her in on the date later on. If she's really a good friend, chances are she'll want to hear all about your experience, despite her hurt feelings.

Friendship Amnesia

I've had the same best friend for five years. We were together all the time until she got a boyfriend. Now she spends every minute she can with him. How do I tell her how I feel?

We've *all* been through this one before! **A friend gets a boyfriend, and bam! she forgets all about her girlfriends**—including your standing date for Saturdays at the mall!

No doubt, it totally sucks when this happens. But, to be fair, balancing boyfriends with friends is always hard. Cut your cutie-obsessed pal some slack.

The bad news is, **some girls can get caught in an all-boyfriend-all-the-time rut**. If your formerly normal pal cancels plans with you to be with her sweetie more than twice in a row—or if she never spends time with you without him, then you'll need to talk to her about it. Be honest, but be direct. Say something like "I'm psyched for you that you have a boyfriend, but you've spent so much time with him that I've been feeling pretty neglected. Let's hang out this weekend, okay?" A little reality check might be all she needs to get back on the friendship track.

Make a Date: Are you worried that your buds are feeling neglected because of all the time you're spending with your new boyfriend? Well, don't just sit there—plan some quality time with your gal pals! Below, we've listed four cool ways to hang out with your girl group. Call all your friends and schedule each date and a time when everyone's available. Write down the time and day you're planning to meet in the space next to each get-together suggestion. Then make a pledge—don't weasel out of your plans with your girls, even if your boyfriend calls to make plans!

1. BARGAIN HUNTER—Plan a trip to the local mall. Decide beforehand that you're only going to spend five, ten, or fifteen dollars. Then see who can find the coolest thing in the mall for that amount of money!

Date	Time
Location	
Girlfriends	

2. TEE FOR YOU—Go mini-golfing with your girl group. The time you spend together is sure to be more fun than a hole in one!

Date	Time
Location	
Girlfriends	

3. GAB AND GLAM—Make simultaneous appointments at the nearest (or cheapest) nail salon and get manicures and pedicures together. Let your girlfriends pick out your polish color for you. Then you pick out theirs!

Date	Time
Location	
Girlfriends	

4. BOWL-O-RAMA—Hang at the local bowling alley and play a few frames together. On the computerized scorecard, make up funny nicknames for each person that say something about their personality—like Sparkle Princess, Play2Win, or Gutterball.

Date	Time
Location	
Girlfriends	

Spontaneous Dislike Disorder

My friend is going out with a hot guy. Every time my friend hangs out with her guy on lunch break, our other friends blow up and say "She always hangs out with him! We can't stand that guy!" They totally don't like him, and it's making life miserable!

So let's say your worst nightmare comes true: **You hate your friend's boyfriend.** We mean big-time dislike. Before you decide to tell her that he's the most annoying person you've ever shared a lunch table with, head to a neutral corner and think about *why* you don't like him.

Reason 1:

Could it be that you're just bummed that she has a sweetie and you don't? If that's it, you should know that it's completely normal for you to feel cranky. But you have to realize that this is not your friend's fault, or her boyfriend's, either. So back off. Give your ego a rest—and give the happy couple a break.

Reason 2:

Suppose you've thought it over, and the fact is, there is something about your friend's boyfriend that turns you off—period. Maybe it's the way he slurps down his food in the cafeteria. Maybe it's because the only thing he can talk about is what happened on *WWF: Smackdown* this week.

Fine. Whatever the reason, you can't be expected to get along with everyone. But if your friend adores this dude, you *can* be expected to respect her feelings, and feel glad that she has found someone who makes her happy.

So, when you're with them, you don't have to act like her boyfriend's best buddy, but you don't have to spit fire at him, either.

(Oh—and next time, try not to shoot him a look that could kill when he snorts rudely at one of your jokes. If your girlfriend is paying attention, she'll do that for you.)

Reason 3:

Red alert! You don't like your girlfriend's guy because in your view **he's totally bad news**. If you get uptight every time he tells her she's a dumb blonde, or when he talks about cutting class, or when he blasts music that totally degrades women, speak up. Sit your pal down and tell her what you think of this guy—and this time, be up front. Explain to her that you're only mentioning your concerns because you really care about her, and you're afraid she's not being given the respect she deserves.

Give her a chance to talk about his good qualities, and what she sees in him. Then reassess your own feelings.

Girlfriend Dos and Don'ts

If you're the one with the honey, here are some ways to stay tight with your gal pals:

Do spend one night of the weekend with your friends, and the other night with your sweetie.

Don't break plans with your girlfriends at the last minute because your guy called with a better offer.

Do let your friends know (through words and actions) that their friendship is special to you.

Don't let your friend put down your boyfriend without an explanation. Talk to her about it. There could a friendship frustration issue hidden behind her dis.

Do remember that your friends might not want to spend every waking moment discussing your boyfriend's best qualities.

Do limit your PDAs when your girlfriends are around. Save serious make-out sessions for when you and your sweetie can snuggle in private.

Don't forget what it's like not to have a boyfriend. Be considerate if your single friend is feeling alone and mopey.

Third Wheel Syndrome

Whenever I go to the mall with my best friend and her boyfriend, they hang all over each other and make out. I feel like an idiot standing there next to them. HELP!

Tempted to break out the air horn and call a PDA (Public Display of Affection) foul on your friend and her man? We don't blame you.

But lots of times, in an effort to make sure she's giving equal time to both her honey and her girls, a friend might try to take care of the issue by hanging out with everyone at the same time. Now, in theory, this is a good idea. But sometimes it just doesn't work out.

Instead of being a part of a group of friends hanging together, **you can end up feeling like some awkward extra in your friend's reenactment of the sappiest scenes from _Titanic_.**

As a single girl faced with the possibility of contracting Third Wheel Syndrome, you need to evaluate your well-meaning friend's invitations on a case-by-case basis. Check out the chart on the following pages to find out when it's safe to hang with the kissing couple, and when to proceed at your own risk.

INVITATION	THE PROS
Your friend's debut as an extra in a Dr. Pepper commercial is on Superbowl Sunday. You and her boyfriend are invited to watch with her family.	You're probably more comfortable with her parents and siblings than he is! So you've got the one-up in this situation.
You had plans to go to the mall with your girlfriend, but now her guy wants to come shopping, too.	Really, *he's* the third wheel here. If you let him tag along today, you might feel more comfortable the next time she brings you on a date with them.
Your best friend's guy is taking her to Pizza Emporium for a veggie supreme, and she asks you to join them.	A casual meal with even the gushiest couple has never ruined a friendship.
Your friend and her honey are heading to a barbecue at his best friend's house. Wanna go?	Even though you're going as a threesome, it is a party. Your friend's guy probably has some cool buddies for you to meet.
She swore she'd see the new Adam Sandler movie with you, but now she wants to invite her sweetie, too.	You're there for the movie, not to chat. So what if your bud's boyfriend's sitting on the other side of her?

THE CONS	COMFORT LEVEL SCALE: 1-10
She might make room for him on the love seat, forcing you to squash between her little brother and Grandma Pearl.	Relax. This situation is a totally comfy **9**. There's no way the two lovebirds will engage in any PDA with her dad in the same room. Which leaves you feeling ultra-cozy.
Watching him compliment her adorable figure in each pair of boot-legs she tries on may make you wish you had a sweet guy along for the ride, too.	**7**. Shopping is more fun as a group activity—he can offer a guy's POV on how that skirt you've been dying for looks on you.
There is the possibility that he may tenderly swipe at the stray drop of tomato sauce on her chin. (Gag!)	**7**. If you're eating a slice at the coolest hangout in town, make sure you're fine with the idea that everyone there will know you're tagging along with the couple of the year.
If you don't know anyone but your pal and her boy, you could be left standing by the chips when they go for a walk.	**5**. This can go either way. You could have a blast with the crowd, or you could be stuck in the corner. Why not be adventurous and go for it?
Darkened movie theaters practically scream "make-out opportunity." They might just take advantage.	**3**. You *could* pretend you can't hear their slurpy kissing noises over the audience laughter, but it also might ruin your good time. Maybe you should suggest she do something else with her honey after the show.

Split Personality

This really popular guy likes my friend, and whenever she's around him, she acts so conceited and I can't stand it! It's like she's a different person!

We all have a girlfriend who's done this: **The minute she's around her guy, her personality does a 180-degree turn.** The change happens instantly, right before your eyes: Her voice goes up an octave, she twirls her hair, she goes from smart and sassy to clueless and catty, and frankly, it makes you feel like projectile vomiting.

The only way to deal with this is to point out (nicely, of course) that when her boyfriend's around your gal pal transforms faster than Madonna's look.

Since you're basically going to say something negative, start off with something positive before you hit her with the criticism.

Try this approach: "I really like Jake. He seems cool, but when you're around him, you act . . . well, strange." If she asks you what you mean, it's best to give concrete examples. For instance, instead of screaming "You act like a total airhead, and it's driving me nuts!" You can say something like "You told him you couldn't figure out the tip at the diner, but when we're out alone, you always handle the math. What's the deal?"

Admitting that she's acting differently for the benefit of her guy will probably be too hard for your friend to handle. So if she chooses to let the conversation drop there, let it—but don't be afraid to say something if the pattern continues.

If something your pal did or said when she was in the presence of her guy was not only out of character but actually hurt your feelings, call her on the insult when you have some alone time. Tell her, "It was really fun hanging out with you and Jake and his friends at Pizza Hut—until you started joking about my braces. It made me feel awful."

START OFF WITH SOMETHING POSITIVE

A Friend in Need

My friend's boyfriend just dumped her, and ever since she hasn't been able to stop thinking about him. She keeps talking about the fun times they had together—and she's not moving on! How can I help her get over him?

It's inevitable: **breakups happen**. And when they do, a heavy dose of time spent with girlfriends is the best cure. When your pal gets dumped (or even if she's cut him loose), she'll need you to comfort her, to reassure her that this was all for the best, and to listen to her analyze and reanalyze what happened every fifteen minutes.

Now you might be tempted to totally trash the guy, but tread lightly in the bad-mouthing territory.

While **a little ex-boyfriend bashing is okay**, it's also possible that the two of them will get back together in a few days. And your friend will, no doubt, be left with the memory of you totally trashing her sweetie.

You also may also want to gloat—saying something like "I knew you shouldn't have let him tongue-kiss you!" But we know you won't act on that instinct. Why? Because if the roles were reversed and you called your friend for sympathy, you'd be devastated if she assaulted you with a barrage of "I told you so"s.

So, **in the event of a breakup emergency**, the best thing you can do is forgive your girlfriend for any minor slipups she may have made while she was head over heels. Remember, *you're* the one who can help your heartbroken bud analyze the situation and figure out what might've gone wrong. *You're* the one who can get her mind off the whole thing by renting wacky Cameron Diaz comedies and giving her a flawless manicure. And *you're* the one who can convince your friend that she will survive the breakup, and eventually find another guy.

After all, no one ever said friendship was about perfection. It's all about forgiveness, support, and caring.

Girls' Night In

Looking for a Friday night pick-me-up? Whether you're nursing your own broken heart or trying to help a friend heal, call all your girlfriends over for a night of girls-only fun. Below are a few theme ideas to inspire you:

1. BEAUTY FEST: Haul out your nail polish, mud masks, hair spray, and glitter, because tonight is all about feeling and looking fabulous (or maybe going a little over-the-top ridiculous with your style). Do each other's nails, sit around slurping fruit smoothies, and give each other hair makeovers (naturally curly girls can get straightened out, and straight girls can get curly). If you're in a wacky mood, go all out with blue eye shadow, red lipstick, stick-on jewels, and false eyelashes. Then, once everyone's feeling fab, just sit around talking, having fun, and admiring what an outrageously glam group you are.

2. SNACK SOIRÉE: Bring the party into the kitchen! Break out some aprons and mixing bowls and whip up a feast. Plan a theme night: Mexican fiesta, Chinese pu-pu platter, vegetarian extravaganza, or top-your-own pizza. Or throw nutrition to the wind (hey, it's only for one night) and have a sweets explosion! Serve ice cream *hors d'oeuvres*, eat brownies for dinner, and bake cookies for dessert!

3. MOVIE SCREENING: Have everyone bring their favorite video and candy. You provide the popcorn (make it the old-fashioned way, in a pot on the stove), the soft drinks, and the comfy couch. Settle in for a long night of marathon viewing.

4. GAME DAY: Ask your girlfriends to come bearing their favorite board game. Good ones include: Mad Libs, Taboo, Trivial Pursuit, Scattergories, Monopoly, and Twister. Or create a little drama (and spooky thrills) by busting out the Ouija board.

6 chapter

Fighting Words

FRIENDSHIP RULE:
Fights happen, so fight fair.

You've tried to carefully maneuver around the bumps and obstacles on the road to friendship—then wham! **Major pileup! You and your friends are having a fight!**

You may give each other the silent treatment, or calmly hash things out in the girl's bathroom, or scream and yell until you both decide to hug and make up. But no matter which route you choose, an argument doesn't have to be a sign that the friendship is over.

The best of friends can survive even the worst of fights (and most times, come through them with their friendship even stronger). In this chapter, we'll tell you how.

Agreeing to Disagree

Every time I get mad at my friend, I'm afraid to tell her, because I don't want to lose the friendship. But then I just get even madder! What can I do?

Maybe the way she always talks about her fabulous new boyfriend has gotten on your last nerve, and you just *have* to let her know it. Or maybe she's tired of you constantly putting down the kind of music she likes and she can't keep it inside any longer. **Go ahead, let it out!** Friendships can't grow if you don't let the other person know how you're feeling. But when you do let loose, use the rules below as guidelines:

1. Talk, rather than shouting or throwing things.

2. Listen. Try to understand where your friend is coming from. To use an old cliché, hear her thoughts on the subject and try to put yourself in her shoes.

3. Take a moment to ask yourself and your friend how important the cause of your argument is. Launching into a shouting match over whose boyfriend is cuter or who should return the black dress you both accidentally bought for the prom is silly—and not all that crucial. If you suspect the topic at hand is being given a little too much attention, try to bring a little humor into the situation. You might want to say something like "Do you realize how silly we sound? It's just a dress. Isn't our friendship more important?"

4. Stay in control of your anger. Don't say anything that you'll regret. No matter what the argument's about, don't resort to low blows like insulting your friend about her braces or her pimple problem. Comments like this won't win the argument for you. They'll just make your bud (and you) feel bad. If you find yourself getting super-mad, and teetering on the verge of getting ugly, walk away. It's better than staying—and possibly doing permanent damage to your friendship.

Your Turn

Fighting with friends

"When friends and I fight, I try to keep my cool and ask myself, 'Is this worth getting all worked up about?' If it is, then I calmly discuss with my friend what's bothering me." **—Gracie**

"When I disagree with my friends, I just tell them. If it's important I'll make an issue out of it, but then I still try to understand their point of view." **—Laura**

"One time a friend and I got very mad at each other over a boy we both liked. We didn't talk for a week. Finally, we couldn't stand not talking to each other, so we discussed why we were so angry and vowed never to argue over a guy again." **—Molly**

Talk and Listen.

69

Fighting Strategies Decoded

Whenever I get into a fight with my friend, she refuses to talk to me. I get so frustrated, but I don't know what to do. Help!

Everyone has her own fight mode—her own way of dealing when things aren't working out right. Some crank up the volume, and others retreat into a cocoon of silence. Here are some of the more popular—though not necessarily effective—ways people deal with anger, and some tips on how to level the playing field.

The Freeze-Out

You're just *not* talking to her. She taps you on the shoulder in homeroom, and **you ignore her**. She turns to chat with you at your side-by-side lockers, and you quickly grab your books and walk away. Every time she tries to approach you, you hightail it out of the room. It's driving her nuts—which is exactly why you're doing it.

WHAT'S GOING ON: We know—you don't want to say a word to her, because you're afraid that if you open your mouth, you'll just end up screaming. But let's get real—the only way you're ever going to solve this disagreement is by talking to your girlfriend.

Besides, how can she apologize for whatever she's wrong about if you won't listen long enough to let her?

MAKE THE FIGHT FAIR: Somehow, you've got to **break the silence**. If you can't bring yourself to actually speak to your friend, write a note. Or say, quickly and quietly, "We need to talk about what's going on with us."

If you're on the other side of this argument, and your friend is the one who's freezing you out, try warming her up by reminding her about the best parts of your friendship. Say something like "I really miss talking with you—can we please discuss this?" If your girlfriend doesn't respond to your first peace attempt, you've got to try again. After your second or third attempt, maybe she'll realize that her silence isn't getting you anywhere, and you two can hash out the problem. But if she still refuses even to look your way when you speak, then you've got to **wait for her to thaw** on her own time.

The Gang-Up

Your best friend is so wrong that you feel the need to **let everyone else in your group know exactly what a jerk she's being**. Then, when someone suggests that everyone meet for pizza after school you say sure, as long as the trip doesn't include the friend you're fighting with.

WHAT'S GOING ON: When you're not sure about something (whether

it's an outfit, a guy, or your choice of elective classes next year), the first thing you do is gather the support of your pals. And that's exactly what you're up to here. You feel totally uncomfortable about fighting with your best friend, so you get everyone you can firmly placed in your corner.

MAKE THE FIGHT FAIR:

It's bad enough that the two of you are on the outs, but alienating your friend from the rest of the group is childish—and just asking for your grudge against each other to grow.

Step back for a second and remind yourself that **this disagreement is between you and your friend**. Talk it out one on one, and don't ask anyone else to get involved.

If you find yourself on the receiving end of this horrible head game, approach your friend and lay it all on the line. Tell her that you want to end this argument, but you want to do it calmly and fairly—between the two of you.

If she doesn't soften up and see how childish she's acting, you may have to face the fact that this friendship means more to you than it does to her. **Friendship is a two-way street.** You both have to want to solve the problem.

The Nitpicker

You and your bud roll up to the drive-through. She orders you your usual—a Diet Coke and small fries. You blow up because, if she had asked you, your friend would have known that today you're hungry, and you wanted the *large* fries!

WHAT'S GOING ON:
Ooooh-kay. Let's acknowledge right now that **this is not about the super size**. There's something bigger happening. So what is it?

MAKE THE FIGHT FAIR:
First, think about exactly when you have been feeling angry with your friend: when she jetted out of school on Friday without asking you if you wanted to catch a ride with her? When you went to the movies and she decided what you should see?

Try to find the common denominator in the little arguments that have been messing up your friendship. (Could you, deep down, be feeling as if your bud doesn't care about what *you* want?) Once you get to the heart of the matter, approach your friend rationally, and tell her how you feel. She may have no idea what the real problem has been all along.

Get to the Heart of the Matter

If you find your friend picking fights for what seem like silly reasons, ask her what's wrong. Say something like "I've noticed you seem upset with me a lot lately. What's bothering you?" By encouraging your bud to vent her true feelings, you will let her know that you sense there's a problem, and you want to fix it.

Both Sides of the Story: If your friend knows you've been thinking about her side of things, she'll be more likely to talk about the problem you're having—and want to make up. We know you want to state your case to her calmly and clearly so she knows where you're coming from. We're here to help.

Use the lines below to write about an argument you had (or are currently having) with one of your friends. Then, on the opposite page, lay down your point of view, and describe how you feel about the argument. Then turn the page, and put yourself in your friend's position. Try to think of what her angers, frustrations, and point of view might be. Write down what she might be thinking. Then share what you've written with the person you're fighting with. Discuss what you wrote and get to the heart of what's really bothering both of you.

We're Fighting About:

_____

_____

_____

_____

_____

_____

_____

A Look at My Side:

A Look at Your Side:

You Fight Right

1 Sure, your best friend stole your boyfriend, but when your mom tells you your friend's cat has feline leukemia, you call your pal to talk to her about it.

2 You two duke it out like Mike Tyson and Oscar de la Hoya, but when you finally resolve things, it makes the friendship stronger.

3 When your pal's bad habits get on your nerves, you're sure to tell her about it—calmly and directly.

4 The last time the two of you got in a screaming fight, your other friend was able to help you sit down and reach a compromise.

5 When your friend complained to you that you were spending way too much time with your guy, you gave it serious thought before agreeing and promising to divide your time better.

6 Last week, you gave her the silent treatment after she told you the death penalty was the best thing that ever happened to the United States. This week, you've both agreed not to discuss politics.

When the Fight Is Finished...

Making Up

Whew! The fight is over, and **you and your pal are best friends again**. Well, almost. You still have to figure out how you're going to deal with the problem that caused your argument in the first place. There are three basic ways you can do that:

1. You can agree to disagree—admit that neither one of you was 100 percent right or wrong—and end the battle cleanly. Before you return to normal friendship mode, promise to be more considerate of each other's point of view in the future.

2. One of you can prove your point so completely that the other actually admits, "You're right, I'm sorry." The "wrong" person will usually promise not to upset her friend by acting the same way or doing the same thing again.

3. One of you can sacrifice your own need to win for the good of the friendship. In other words, even though you're not absolutely sure she's right, you swallow your pride and tell her she is—just to end the fight.

Choice 3 is obviously the quickest way to end any disagreement—and even though it may seem as though you're giving in and admitting defeat, it's really **the most mature move** you can make in some situations.

Say your bud's angry because she thinks that you've been ignoring her in favor of more face time with your honey. But you think you've been devoting plenty of Q.T. to the friendship, and don't understand why she can't see that. After realizing that your friend's never going to see things your way, you decide to end the discussion with a simple "I'm sorry" or "Your friendship means a lot to me, and I don't want to fight anymore."

What you're really doing here is prioritizing—putting your valued friendship before your need to prove your point. You realize that it's less important to win the battle than it is to lose one of the most important people in your life—your girlfriend.

I'm sorry

You mean a lot to me

Let's not fight over this anymore

Choosing Sides

Disagreeing with one girlfriend at a time is hard enough. But what happens when you're **caught between bickering buds?** Well, things can get ugly fast. You may find yourself called as a witness for the prosecution *and* the defense in your girlfriends' own episode of *The Practice*.

Our advice? Before you're forced to testify, stop and think about whether this situation really involves you at all. If it doesn't, plead the Fifth. Declare yourself Switzerland. In other words, *stay neutral*. But feel free to lend an ear and be supportive of both your friends.

When they each come crying to you about what's going on, your job is to be sympathetic and impartial. Let your feuding friends know that while you'll listen to each side of the story, you *won't* listen to one badmouth the other.

If you think you can help the two resolve things, turn on your persuasive charm and get your feuding friends to sit down together. Tell each girlfriend that they're important to you and that you would really like to see them work out their problems. With you as an **impartial mediator**, they might be willing to talk out their differences.

If, on the other hand, you decide to take the side of one friend over the other, be aware of the risks—there's a chance you could lose the person you're not siding with as a pal—for good.

The Breakup

Okay, so you and your gang have survived competitions over boys, jealousy, and a couple of humongous fights. You've come out of it all with a strong, amazing friendship. The whole group of you can finish each other's sentences. You spend time planning your futures together. You rely on each other for support and encouragement. It's unthinkable that ***one day you and your close friends might break up***—right?

Unfortunately, even the tightest group of friends can wind up going their separate ways (and it's usually no one's fault when it happens). People move away, people's view of life changes, and people grow apart. Whatever the reason, here are some of the ways a split can go down, and how you can cope with each one.

The Drift

Otherwise known as a mutual parting of the ways, this split doesn't involve screaming, slamming phones, or massive fights. It's just that, well, maybe your interests have changed. Or, since your pal joined the cheerleading squad, she spends her afternoons and weekends practicing pyramids and splits, while you're touring the city with your choir group.

Maybe you've come to disagree on what makes for a good time—your girlfriend is into following your hometown indie rock band from gig to gig, while you'd rather hang at the park picking up blading tips from a cute skater boy. What it comes down to is that **you and your girlfriend simply don't have much in common anymore**.

HOW TO DEAL:
While it's totally bittersweet, this is the easiest, least painful breakup to go through. You slowly realize that you have more fun when you're not hanging out with your girlfriend. So you stop calling each other as much, find different people to catch a ride home with, and no longer have standing weekend plans.

It may feel a little weird at first, but that's normal. Drifting apart from your group means you're growing, changing . . . that's just a part of life. And hey, if you have a sudden crisis, or get the internship at the local radio station that you've been dreaming of since you were ten, it's okay to call your old buds and share the news. After all, you don't hate each other, you've just moved on.

The Dump

You know how a boy can break up with a girl for no apparent reason? He just stops calling, avoids her in the hallways, and pretty much acts as if there were never a relationship between them? Well, the truth is, girls sometimes do the same thing to each other.

HOW TO DEAL:
If you're the victim of such a breakup (otherwise known as the Dumpee), it can take a while to realize what's happening.

Then, one day, you'll notice that you haven't gotten a call from your friends in a few days—and you'll realize that **they've been hanging out together—without you!**

When this realization hits, don't freak out. It's worth a shot to confront your friend (or group of friends) about their absence. Try saying something like "So you guys rented *American Pie* Saturday night? How come you didn't call me? I would've loved to watch it with you." Give them a chance to tell you straight up what's going on.

But if your pals are regularly leaving you stranded on the sidelines, the brutal reality is, it's time to find a new gang. We know that this hurts. We also realize that you may feel like you've been dumped because you're not a good friend. Hey! It's not about that. Maybe your interests were too different from your group's.

Whatever the reason, don't let it get you down! You ARE a valuable friend—and you deserve to hang with a group of girl-friends who appreciate you and include you because they want to, not because they feel like they have to. (You'll find the right group for you soon enough—don't worry.).

The Blowout

Maybe your friend never showed up to your birthday party. Maybe she spread rumors about you and her brother that weren't true. Or maybe she made a completely inappropriate comment about your cousin's nose job at your family barbecue. Whatever the offense, you are mad. You just can't bear to be nice to a girl who was so inconsiderate of your feelings—and **this friendship is so over**.

HOW TO DEAL:

In this case, the best way to end the friendship is to make a clean break. Whether you let her have it on your front porch, reciting a laundry list of mindless offenses she's committed, or whether you write her a letter explaining why you just don't think you can be friends anymore, you've got to lay it all down for her. To be honest, you'll be totally relieved that you did. And who knows? **Maybe she'll change** the way she treats her friends and you two could end up back together.

Together Again?

Even the worst of breakups doesn't mean that the friendship is over forever. No one knows what the future brings, and in a couple of months—or even years—you and your ex-bud may cross paths again, and decide to **rebuild the friendship**. Hey, even if you don't, that's okay. Because every time a pal makes an exit, it leaves room for another new, amazing friend to enter.

Whether you've moved to a new town or broken up with your old girl group, what do you do when you find yourself in need of a brand-new group of gal pals? Check out chapter 8 to find out.

RENT IT, SEE IT, LIVE IT:

Foxfire (1996/R). After drama and trouble, Maddy and her friends finally decide that they just can't be friends with Legs (Angelina Jolie) anymore.

Getting Friendly

> **FRIENDSHIP RULE:**
> True girlfriends like you for who
> you are—so when you're making
> new friends don't be afraid to
> be yourself!

Maybe you've moved to a new town and don't know anyone. Or maybe you've switched schools and have to work your way into a new crowd. Or maybe you've lived in the same town your entire life, but this year all your close pals are off to private school, leaving you to navigate the hallways of your public school alone. Whatever the situation—**you're in need of some friendly faces**.

Don't panic. Making new friends is not as tough, or as scary, as it sounds. Don't believe us? Check out the info in this chapter.

Sure-fire Places to Find Friends

Okay, so you have no friends. At least, none in the immediate vicinity. We admit it—a situation like this can make you want to curl up on your couch with a stack of your favorite movies and sulk. But—news flash!—you're not going to meet any potential friends in your living room! The only way to find new girlfriends is to **get out of the house** and meet new people. Come on—give it a shot. We've listed six great places to meet, mingle, and get to know below.

---

1. AFTER-SCHOOL ACTIVITIES. Think about what you like to do in your free time and find an activity that centers on that. Do you like to write? Join the school newspaper or yearbook staff. Are you a closet actor or shower singer? Try out for the school play or join the choir. You'll automatically have stuff in common with the people who are already members—which means you'll have a head start when you decide to get friendly!

2. THE LOCAL COFFEE SHOP/FOOD-RELATED HANGOUT. Ever notice how everyone flocks to the pizza joint, the ice cream parlor, the café, or the food court? It's because food is social. And if you're looking to make friends, social is good. Bring a book or magazine to glance at if you don't want to seem like you're weirdly scoping out the crowd. Or, if you're ultra-shy, think about getting a part-time job at one of these places. That way, you'll *have* to talk to people to get your job done— and maybe you'll meet some new girlfriends in the process.

3. HIGH SCHOOL VARSITY B-BALL AND FOOTBALL GAMES. Does the whole town rally around the home team when they compete? Join in! And feel free to comment about the game to the varsity fan sitting next to you.

GO TEAM!

4. THE MUSIC STORE. This is a prime spot to strike up a conversation. After all, who doesn't like to talk about their favorite bands? Jet over to the music store in town, or at the mall, and walk the aisles. If you spot a potential girlfriend shuffling through the Sarah McLaughlin CD, and you're a huge fan yourself, head on over and start some music-related conversation.

5. VOLUNTEER GROUPS. Check out what community service groups in your area are doing, and then sign yourself up. It's likely that there will be lots of people from your school doing the exact same thing. Think about the local animal shelter, senior citizen center, or soup kitchen. Not only will you be making friends, but by donating your time to these worthy causes, you'll be making a difference.

6. CHURCH OR SYNAGOGUE– or wherever your religion takes you. Almost every religious organization has a youth group. Part of the point of that group is to provide a place where teens with similar interests can get together and get to know each other. Amen to that!

RENT IT, SEE IT, LIVE IT:

Now and Then (1995/PG-13). Five unlikely friends (Demi Moore, Rosie O'Donnell, Rita Wilson, Julianne Moore, and Melanie Griffith) find themselves bonded to one another from childhood through the birth of their own children.

Breaking the Ice

Okay, so you've put yourself in situations where there are new people to meet. Now all you have to do is talk to them.

Granted, going up to a group of four girls alone can be an intimidating prospect. (Of course, if you feel bold enough to do it, go for it, girl.) But maybe you'd be more comfortable approaching a potential pal when she's by herself. Wait until she's standing at her locker, in the lunch line, or waiting around to talk to a teacher after class. Then move in.

So here you are . . . standing face-to-face with a potential girlfriend. You want to sound cool, but **what do you say?** Hey, you don't have to invent something ultrahip right on the spot! Cheat a little—we won't tell. Have a few icebreakers in your head before you open your mouth. (It sounds corny, but it works!) Check out the icebreakers below and choose your favorites!

Icebreaker #1: A compliment will get 'em every time.

Say you walked into Starbucks and spotted someone from your gym class. You stand next to her on line, but after your initial "hey" you're not sure what to say. That's when you notice the supercool skirt she's wearing. At this point, it's perfectly legit to say something like "Hey, I really love that skirt—where did you get it?"

It's bound to jump-start a conversation because she's

guaranteed to respond well to someone who's telling her her style is fab. Continue the chat by asking her where she likes to shop, whether she's ever gone to the monthly flea market, or the cool boutiques. If you two really connect, you might even end up with a shopping partner next weekend!

Icebreaker #2: Be honest.

Sometimes the simple approach is best. So if you're in an environment where you're feeling tongue-tied, admit it. Walk up to a friendly-looking person and say "Hi. I'm feeling kind of weird—I don't know anybody here." Sure, you're playing the sympathy card—hoping the other person will take pity on you and hang with you. But the hard-core fact is—this works! Only the most heartless of strangers would ignore you in this situation. So go for it!

Maybe all this sounds like no prob to you. Or maybe you're sitting there thinking, "Are they nuts? No way am I going to go up to some strange girl and make conversation!" Well, we wouldn't make you look stupid. Ever. By opening yourself up to new places, experiences, and people, you'll find girlfriends who are right for you. Guaranteed.

Some people are naturally outgoing, and some need to work at meeting new people. What's your deal? Find out below.

Keep track of how many times you answer "A", "B", or "C" to get your score.

1 You see the new girl in school walking to class alone. You:

   A. rush up to her and ask what she's doing Friday night.

   B. grab your best friend and approach the new girl together, to see if she needs directions to the gym or anything.

   C. smile and keep walking to your locker.

2 Your math teacher asks for volunteers to stand at the blackboard and demonstrate problem five from your homework assignment. You spent hours last night figuring that one out perfectly, so you:

   A. immediately raise your hand and say "I'll do it!"

   B. look around, and when you notice that no one else has raised their hand, offer to do it yourself.

   C. sit there quietly, hoping you don't get called on.

3 At a party, you see your crush from social studies, standing alone in front of the snack table. You decide to:

   A. go up to him and say "Hey, you're in my history class, right?"

B. slowly make your way to his side, then stand there for a few minutes before saying hi.

C. take a few minutes to mentally list the pros and cons of approaching him, then chicken out.

4 On your way home from school, a girl you vaguely recognize from biology stops to ask directions to Trina's Treasures, a local thrift shop. You don't know, so you:

A. spend ten minutes explaining that while you can't get her to Trina's Treasures, you *can* point her in the direction of Secondhand Rose, the coolest vintage shop within the county limits.

B. tell her you aren't sure how to get there, but that the gas station on the corner of Main and Chestnut has Chamber of Commerce maps.

C. smile and say you don't know, sorry.

5 After school you scoop ice cream at Fred and Ethel's in town. When a group of kids from your school comes in wearing face paint in the school colors, you say:

A. "Hey, you guys came from the pep rally, right? I've been dying to know—was the mascot's act as funny as it was last year?"

B. "How's it going? Did you just come from the pep rally?"

C. "Hi, do you guys know what you want?"

Scoring

Mostly A's—Way out there

There's no way you'll ever be caught without friends for very long. You take advantage of a solo situation (like being stuck at a party by yourself) and turn it into a meet-and-greet opportunity. It's cool that you are outgoing and chatty, but remember not to overwhelm potential pals (who might be a bit more shy) with your superfriendly ways.

Mostly B's—Out and about

You know when to swallow your nervousness and be social, but you do have a quiet, shy side to you as well, which makes for a great balance! While you may not launch right into a friendly conversation with a total stranger, you are probably really good at sending out friendly vibes, which hint at your social nature.

Mostly C's—In your shell

Yeah, we know. It can be really hard to open up and talk to people, especially when you have to make the first move, but you can do it! Just ease into it. Start by talking to acquaintances in class or at an after-school club, and then work yourself up to the bolder stuff, like showing up at a party by yourself. The more you do it, the easier it gets. We promise.

Common (and Uncommon!) Denominators

Meeting new people is only the first step in building friend-ships. Next you have to figure out which people you'd really like to get to know.

See, new girlfriends are kind of like boyfriends: You strike up a relationship because you are immediately attracted to something about that person—whether it's her remarkable confidence, her easy-going nature, her sense of humor, or her cool insights on one of your shared interests.

But while common interests may spark a friendship, don't freak out if, somewhere along the way, you realize that your new pal isn't the spitting image of yourself. Once you get beyond your shared enthusiasm for the newest boy band, you may discover that you and your friend are pretty different.

That's okay! Because a **terrific friendship is also about learning from the other person.**

Say you'd never even considered going to a James Bond flick, but your pal is an expert on all things 007. Why not check out a couple of old movies with her? Even if you don't become a card-carrying member of the Bond Fan Club, you are opening yourself up to new experiences, and seeing things from your friend's perspective.

Then, the next time she suggests a movie marathon, you can fill her in on the fact that Cameron Crowe was making amazing films long before *Jerry Maguire* and *Almost Famous* ever hit the big screen. Invite her over to watch *Say Anything*. Add popcorn, and watch the friendship blossom.

Friendship Builders

It may sound cheesy, but one of the coolest parts of a new friendship is the intense, getting-to-know-you conversations you'll have. If you're in a silly mood, there are tons of fun games you can play to get to know each other better.

1. TOP FIVE MOVIES OF ALL TIME. Go ahead, list yours first. Then tell your new friend why you chose those movies. Reverse the process and learn something cool about your new bud.

MY FAVORITES:
1.
2.
3.
4.
5.

YOUR FAVORITES:

1. --
2. --
3. --
4. --
5. --

2. IF YOU WERE STRANDED ON A DESERT ISLAND . . . Ask your new girlfriend what she would bring along. It's an interesting way to learn what's most important to her. Then you can share what you'd need to survive.

3. BEST DAY/WORST DAY OF YOUR LIFE. This one's a little more intense, so you should probably save it for a time when you feel you and your new girlfriend are really starting to get close. Begin with the best day. (Maybe it's the day your parents told you you were going to have a little brother. Or maybe it's when you performed the lead in the school play.) Give your bud the full details about what happened. Then ask for her best experience. After you've shared giggles and smiles over happy times, it's okay to get into the heavier stuff, if you want.

4. WHAT WOULD YOU DO IF. . . ? Hypothetical situations are always fun, and can reveal a lot about a person. Have your friend answer these questions:

❓ What would you do if your crush asked you out?

❓ What would you do if the world was going to blow up in twenty-four hours?

❓ What would you do if you were never allowed to drive?

❓ What would you do if you could switch places with anyone in the world?

❓ What would you do if you had the choice between spending the day with your favorite boy band or winning a million dollars?

See how easy that was? Once you get past the "What if nobody likes me?" fear, making friends is pretty simple—and fun.

So what happens when you find out your newest, best girlfriend is facing a truly tough time? You support her in any way you can. Read on to find out how.

9 chapter

Friend 911

> ### FRIENDSHIP RULE:
> A good friend can really make
> a difference when you're dealing
> with tough issues.

When you're really tight with your buds, you can sense when something's wrong with one of them. Maybe they're anxious about a big test, or stressed about their upcoming swim meet, or just cranky in general. Those problems are easy to fix, and as a good friend, you know how to fix them.

But what happens if **you suspect that something serious is going on** with one of your girlfriends? What if your pal is struggling with some *really* tough issues, like depression, an eating disorder, or drug abuse? None of these problems is very easy to talk about—especially when your friend doesn't even think there is a problem. **You want to help**—you care too much about her to ignore the situation—but you're not sure how.

We've come up with three steps you can take to come to the aid of your girlfriend if you suspect she's in trouble:

1. TELL HER YOU'RE CONCERNED. Chances are, since you spend so much time with your girlfriend, you're the first one who's noticed that something's up with her. And even if she hasn't admitted having a problem, she'll probably open up to you sooner than she would to her parents or a teacher. So the very first thing you can do to help is talk to her. Be straight-forward, but not accusatory. Say something like "I really care about you and I'm worried that you're not OK. I'm here if you want to talk about *anything*."

Be careful not to put your friend on the defensive—especially since whatever is bothering her is probably making her feel really vulnerable right now.

Instead, hang back and **give her a chance to open up** and tell you the problem. *Don't* guess at it yourself. For example, don't say something like "Are you doing drugs?" or "I think you have an eating disorder." If you guess wrong, you could upset your

Hang back & give her a chance to open up.

friend and cause her to shut you out. Instead, try something more general, like "I've noticed that you haven't been yourself lately," or "You seem really run down. What's going on?" The goal is to let her know that you're on her side. You're there to help, not to punish or accuse or force her to talk.

And no matter what she does say, **don't judge her**. For example, if she admits that she hasn't been eating lately, don't exclaim "That's anorexia! Do you have any idea how bad that is for your body?" Instead, let her know you want to find a way to get her some help for her problem.

It might seem like it would be easier to approach your troubled pal along with one or two mutual friends, but that's actually not a great idea. Your friend might feel like you're all ganging up on her, which is a situation sure to make her close herself off. (It's also not a good move, at first, to tell others that you think your pal has a problem. After all, your hunch could be wrong.) Keep your concerns to yourself, and **talk to your friend alone**.

Listen hard to what she's saying. If she's denying a problem, ask yourself if you could have misinterpreted the signs of trouble you've been seeing. If necessary, casually ask someone else if they've noticed the same differences in your friend that you have.

2. AFTER YOUR INITIAL CHAT, CHECK IN WITH YOUR PAL A FEW DAYS LATER. Ask her how she's doing. If she's admitted to you that she has a problem, ask if she's taken any of the steps you two talked about to get help. If she hasn't, rehash the options you

discussed. Ask her if she'll promise to talk to someone about her problem by Friday (or some other day). Set a specific time for her to get help by—she's actually more likely to stick to the plan that way. If your friend won't admit there's a problem at all, mention again that you are worried about her, and this time explain why. ("You don't seem to be eating too much"; "You've got a lot of bruises on your arms.") Offer to help her through whatever it is she's dealing with, every step of the way.

Whether or not she admits her problem, **provide her with the tools to get help**. Assure your pal that whatever her problem is, it's certainly nothing to be embarrassed about. Find some hotline numbers she can call (we'll give you some good ones later on in this chapter), help her locate a therapist, and even offer to go with her to the appointment if she's nervous or scared.

3. IF YOUR PAL WON'T ADMIT SHE HAS A PROBLEM, OR WON'T GET HELP, TELL SOMEONE ELSE ABOUT IT. Before you talk to anyone, tell your friend that you're still extremely concerned and that you think you should get an adult involved. Your friend may not like this idea, but if she's in serious danger (e.g., she's suicidal, hasn't been eating for days, or is being abused by a boyfriend or family member), you need to tell someone who can do something about the situation. This person should be an adult (not another friend) that both you and she trust. Potential confidants include: your mom or dad,

one or both of her parents, another friend's parents, a coach, a teacher, or a guidance counselor.

Here's the really rough part: Even if your friend makes you promise not to tell anyone about her problem, you've got to tell an adult anyway.

But don't do it behind her back. Instead, let her know that you disagree with her wishes, and that you are taking matters into your own hands. Say something like "I know you may be mad at me now, but I am really worried about you and I don't want anything bad to happen to you. I think it would help if an adult knew about this problem." That way, there's no way she can say you're betraying her trust.

7 Things to Say to Comfort a Friend in Crisis

1 "If you need to talk, let me know."

2 "I'm sorry that you're going through this."

3 "I really care about you, and if you need my help, just ask."

4 "None of this changes how I feel about you. You're one of my best friends."

5 "I understand if you need to be alone for a while."

6 "If talking to my mom will help you, you can totally do that, you know."

7 "Whatever you need from me—a hug, a joke, or a frozen mochaccino—I can deliver."

Family Matters

There are so many reasons that stress could be happening in one of your friend's homes. A parent or sibling could have a life-threatening disease, her parents could be talking about divorce, there could be alcohol or drug-related problems in the family. There might even be issues with infidelity.

Whatever the difficulty, when times get tough at home, your friend will probably not act like her usual self. She might be stressed out and depressed, and might not want (or be able) to hang out as often. She might not be as chatty on the phone, or as gung-ho about gossiping at school.

This is when you get to give your love and support to someone you truly care about—someone who needs it badly—in a way that only girlfriends can. Your main objective is to **be there for your pal in whatever way she needs you most**. If she wants to talk about what's going on at home, lend an ear. But if you sense she doesn't want to discuss the situation, tell her that's cool, and ask if there's anything you can do for her. For example, if her mom is sick, her family might need help around the house. Offer

104

to shop for groceries or to take their dog for a walk. Even doing the smallest things can lighten your friend's load. Not to mention the fact that it will make your pal feel better just knowing that you're there, ready and waiting to do anything for her.

On the other hand, maybe she needs to be distracted from the situation. Maybe she needs a reminder that, even though she's struggling with some tough stuff right now, she's still your number-one partner in crime. So, if in the middle of a deep conversation she starts talking about the latest episode of *Popular*, that's your signal to go ahead and dish with her. She might not want to talk about her problems just then. Also, don't be afraid to ask if she wants to go to the mall or movies to get her mind off things. If she doesn't feel like it—or can't leave her family right now—she'll let you know.

Love and Loss

My friend's dog got run over by a car, and now all she does is cry in school. I don't understand why she can't get ahold of herself, but maybe it's because I never had a pet.

Whether it's her trusty Border collie or a favorite grandparent who's recently passed away, it won't be easy for your friend to deal with the death of someone she loves. Everyone reacts to death in different ways: Your pal may not want to mention it at all, or she may cry nonstop and want to talk about it all the time. Instead of trying to guess what would comfort their pal, good girlfriends *ask*. Say something like "I just want you to know that I'm here for you. Let me know what I can do to make things easier for you."

Another idea is to surprise your pal by doing something for her that you know she'll like. For example, bake a batch of her favorite brownies and bring them over. Or, if she really likes Sting, buy her the one CD of his that she doesn't have. A gesture like that will show her that you're thinking of her. We know it sounds goofy, but it really is the *thought* that counts.

RENT IT, SEE IT, LIVE IT:

Fried Green Tomatoes (1991/PG). Evelyn Couch (Kathy Bates) is miserable, and no one seems to take her seriously—until she meets Ninny Threadgoode (Jessica Tandy), a friend who teaches her how to be happy.

Call Me: Sometimes you find yourself totally down, or really stressed about something that's going on in your life. That's okay—we've all been there. But what happens when you have a serious problem on your hands?

You need to fall back on your friends and family for support. (Hey—don't feel weird about it! That's what they're there for!) Use the space below to list friends, family members, teachers—anyone you think you'd feel comfortable talking to when you're feeling bad. If you have the person's phone number, jot it down next to his or her name. Then, if you ever find yourself stuck in a really difficult place, turn to this page, find one of the people you listed, and *tell them about it!*

Friend:	Phone Number:

Professional Help

Lately I've noticed that my friend hasn't been eating very much. She always talks about how fat she thinks she is. But actually, she's really skinny! I think she might have an eating disorder. What should I do?

When a friend is facing a serious issue—any serious issue—it's always a good idea to go to the pros for advice. Make a list of hotlines that specialize in the problem your friend is dealing with. Then call the numbers you find to get more information for yourself on how to approach her. You can ask the counselor working the hotline for literature to give to your friend about her problem. Many hotlines will even tell you how you can find a therapist in your area.

Finally, some crisis intervention hotlines give on-the-spot counseling that can help you and/or your pal immediately if the situation is totally serious and you can't wait to make an appointment with a counselor.

HOTLINE RESOURCE GUIDE

GENERAL

National Youth Crisis Hotline
800-448-4663
This is a twenty-four-hour hotline for any crisis—from pregnancy to drugs to depression.

DRUG ABUSE

DrugHelp National Helplines Network
800-378-4435
Sponsored by the American Council on Drug Education, this twenty-four-hour hotline provides crisis counseling and information on specific drugs and treatment options as well as referrals to treatment programs. It also connects you to support groups and crisis centers nationwide.

National Drug and Alcohol Treatment Hotline
800-662-HELP
When you call this hotline, you hook into a staff of trained counselors who can answer questions, and give out information on alcohol and drug abuse. They can also give you referrals to treatment centers in your area.

CHILD ABUSE/DOMESTIC ABUSE

National Child Abuse Hotline
800-422-4453
This hotline is run by the nonprofit group ChildHelp USA. You can get crisis counseling on sexual abuse, domestic violence,

and rape. They can also recommend therapists, treatment programs, shelters, and legal assistance.

National Domestic Violence Hotline
800-799-SAFE
When you call this twenty-four-hour hotline, you can get crisis counseling and referrals to shelters and transitional housing in your area for victims of domestic violence.

SUICIDE/RUNAWAYS

Covenant House Adolescent Crisis Intervention and Counseling Nineline
800-999-9999
This religiously-affliated twenty-four-hour hotline gives crisis counseling, referrals, and information services to homeless, runaway, and other troubled youth.

National Runaway Switchboard and Suicide Hotline
800-621-4000
Another twenty-four-hour hotline for runaways.

EATING DISORDERS

Eating Disorders Awareness and Prevention
800-931-2237
Trained EDAP staff members will answer questions about eating disorders, give advice on dealing with food and body image issues, and help you find a counselor or therapist.

Harvard Eating Disorders Center
888-236-1188

A national organization dedicated to research and education about eating disorders, the Harvard Center can give you information on how to tell if someone has an eating disorder, how to prevent disorders, and how to go about finding treatment.

MENTAL HEALTH

The Renfrew Center
800-RENFREW

This is a women's mental health center that specializes in the treatment of eating disorders. (The center also deals with anxiety, depression, and substance abuse.) Their hotline provides information and referrals to eating disorder specialists in the United States and Canada.

National Institute of Mental Health
Anxiety Disorders Education Program
888-826-9438

This automated line gives you written information about phobias and depression as well as panic, obsessive-compulsive, general anxiety, and post-traumatic stress disorders.

RAPE/SEXUAL ABUSE

RAINN—Rape, Abuse, Incest National Network
800-656-HOPE

A twenty-four-hour hotline, RAINN offers confidential crisis counseling, particularly for someone who's suffered from sexual assault who cannot reach a rape crisis center through a local call.

Voices in Action
800-7-VOICE-8
This Chicago-based hotline provides international listings for treatment and support for survivors of incest and childhood sexual abuse.

SELF-INJURY

SAFE Alternatives (Self Abuse Finally Ends)
at Rock Creek Center
800-DON'T-CUT
This hotline provides information and treatment referrals for teens and adults who participate in deliberate, repeated self-injurious behavior (like cutting).

SEXUALITY

Gay and Lesbian National Hotline
888-THE-GLNH
Staffed by trained volunteers, the GLNH offers counseling and referrals to people who are dealing with sexuality issues.

Remember, when your friend has a serious problem, you shouldn't keep it a secret for long. Seek help from a professional as early as possible. In the end, your girlfriend will be glad you did.

10 chapter

Friends Forever

Maybe you and your best friend each picked up a copy of this book to celebrate your awesome friendship. Or maybe you're reading it because you're having a fight with your buds and you're not sure what to do. Maybe you're worried that lately, all the members of your girl gang don't seem to be getting along. Or maybe you just wanted some tips on how to make your close friendships even better.

Whatever the reason, we hope this book has showed you the way to have (and be) the best girlfriend in the world. Stick this book on your shelf and look at it any time you're hanging out with your pals, or when you're faced with a friendship dilemma. Like a good girlfriend, it will be there for you whenever you need it.

And, hey, now that we think about it, there's been a kind of a theme running through this book. Here's the Cliff's Notes version:

There are **five qualities** that make our relationships with our girlfriends ultra meaningful, and unlike any other relationship we have throughout

113

our lives. If you and your buds can find and foster these things in your friendships, you'll be girlfriends forever!

1. TRUST. You should be able to trust a pal with anything, from the most serious details of your life (like the argument your parents had that you overheard) to the most embarrassing (like the time you tripped and fell in front of your crush). Your friends are the best people to share your secrets, hopes, and feelings with—things that you could never tell anyone else—because your friends would never tell, either.

2. LOYALTY. Outside your family, your friends are the people you can always depend on to be there for you—on your best and especially your worst days. Girlfriends are allies; they stand by you no matter what. When you're happy, they're happy. When you're not, they'll do anything to cheer you up. And you'd do the same for them in a flash.

3. R-E-S-P-E-C-T. Good girlfriends are on even turf, which means that you respect them and they respect you—everything about you, including your privacy, your family, your goals, your opinions, your differences, and your stuff (even your extensive Barbie collection). And if you're extremely upset and need to be alone, a good girlfriend respects your space, too.

4. GROWTH. As time goes by, people grow and change, and so do their friendships. The strongest ones will grow and evolve along with you. Girlfriends understand that your interests might change from roller skating to scoping out cute guys at the mall on Saturdays. Maybe one year you see a pal in class every day, but the next, you change schools and see her only once a week. Does that mean that your friendship's not as strong or as tight as it used to be? Absolutely not. You can feel close to a girlfriend whether you talk every day or once a month, whether you meet at the park or the food court.

5. UNDERSTANDING. Girlfriends just get it. They understand how you feel and what you're going through. When something's weighing on your mind, it takes a load off just to talk about it with your girlfriends. After all, *they* know why having a zit in the middle of your forehead on Friday night is a major tragedy. *They* know why having to make it home by midnight when you've just started talking to your crush at a party can depress you for the rest of the weekend. And last, but certainly not least, girlfriends give you perspective. They help you see the big picture outside yourself, beyond the zit and Cinderella curfew. With your girlfriends by your side, you can make it through anything!

GIRLFRIENDS JUST GET IT

Friends in the Future: Now that you've finished this book, you and your girlfriends are ready to head off into the sunset. But where will the road take you? Use the lines below and on the following pages to fill in your name, and the names of all your friends. Then look down the column and answer the questions to the right. Give the book to each one of your friends and have them do the same!

> **a.** Where will you go to college?
> **b.** What kind of career will you have?
> **c.** Who will you marry?
> **d.** To what exotic locations will you travel?
> **e.** Will you have children? How many?
> **f.** Where will you live?

Save the predictions to look back on in the days, months, and years to come!

My Name:

a.

b.

c.

d.

e.

f.

Name: _____

a. _____

b. _____

c. _____

d. _____

e. _____

f. _____

Name: _____

a. _____

b. _____

c. _____

d. _____

e. _____

f. _____

Name: _____

a. _____

b. _____

c. _____

d. _____

e. _____

f. _____

III

BOOKS...
FOR THE TIMES
OF YOUR LIFE

0-06-440871-X

How to Be Gorgeous
**The Ultimate Beauty Guide
to Makeup, Hair, and More**
By Elizabeth Brous, former beauty director of **seventeen**

It's **seventeen's** guide to looking glam . . .
so don't delay! It's your turn to be gorgeous!

0-06-447235-3

The Boyfriend Clinic
**The Final Word on Flirting,
Dating, Guys, and Love**
By Melanie Mannarino, senior editor
of **seventeen**. Do you have questions
about love and relationships?
Relax—**seventeen's** got you covered.

0-06-440872-8

Total Astrology
**What the Stars Say About
Life and Love**
By Georgia Routsis Savas
Packed with information about
all the signs in the zodiac. For help
answering your deepest questions—
look to the stars!

0-06-440873-6

Trauma-Rama
**Life's Most Embarrassing
Moments . . .
and How to Deal**
By Megan Stine
Packed with real-life dating,
clothing, family, and friendship
disasters...plus advice on how
to deal if they happen to you!

Available wherever books are sold.

Books created and produced by Parachute Publishing, L.L.C., distributed by HarperCollins Children's Books, a division of HarperCollins Publishers.
© 2001 PRIMEDIA Magazines, Inc., publisher of **seventeen**. **Seventeen** is a registered trademark of PRIMEDIA Magazines Finance Inc.